Rest Beside the Weary Road

Rest Beside the Weary Road

A.M. Watson

Copyright © 2025 by A. M. Watson

Winds of Liberty Publishing

All rights reserved.

No portion of this publication may be reproduced, distributed, or transmitted in any form or by any means, including photocopying, recording, or other electronic or mechanical methods, without the prior written permission from the author, except in the case of brief quotations embodied in reviews and certain other noncommercial uses permitted by U.S. copyright law.

No artificial intelligence (AI) was used in the writing of this work. The author expressly prohibits any entity from using this publication to train AI technologies to generate text, including, without limitation, technologies capable of generating works in the same style or genre as this publication. The author reserves all rights to license uses of this work for generative AI training and development of machine learning language models.

This is a work of historical fiction. Unless otherwise indicated, all the names, characters, businesses, places, events and incidents in this book are either the product of the author's imagination or used in a fictitious manner. Any resemblance to actual persons, living or dead, is purely coincidental.

All Scripture is taken from the King James Bible.

Cover Design: Mountain Peak Edits and Design

ASIN: B0DX7H7DMQ

Paperback ISBN: 979-8-9939542-0-2

For those who left their homes and firesides in defense of their country. Deo Vindice.

"What a cruel thing is war; to separate and destroy families and friends, and mar the purest joys and happiness God has granted us in this world; to fill our hearts with hatred instead of love for our neighbours, and to devastate the fair face of this beautiful world! I pray that, on this day when only peace and good-will are preached to mankind, better thoughts may fill the hearts of our enemies and turn them to peace."

General Robert E. Lee

"It came upon a midnight clear,
That glorious song of old,
From angels bending near the earth,
To touch their harps of gold;
"Peace on the earth, good will to men,
From Heav'n's all-gracious King."
The world in solemn stillness lay,
To hear the angels sing.

Still through the cloven skies they come
with peaceful wings unfurled,
and still their heavenly music floats
o'er all the weary world;
above its sad and lowly plains,
they bend on hovering wing,
and ever o'er its Babel sounds
the blessed angels sing.

Yet with the woes of sin and strife
The world has suffered long;
Beneath the angel strain have rolled
Two thousand years of wrong;
And man, at war with man, hears not
The love-song which they bring;
Oh, hush the noise, ye men of strife
And hear the angels sing.

And ye, beneath life's crushing load,
Whose forms are bending low,
Who toil along the climbing way
With painful steps and slow,
Look now! for glad and golden hours
Come swiftly on the wing.
Oh, rest beside the weary road,
And hear the angels sing!"

For lo! the days are hast'ning on,
By prophet seen of old,
When with the ever-circling years
Shall come the time foretold
When Christ shall come and all shall own
The Prince of Peace, their King,
And saints shall meet Him in the air,
And with the angels sing."
       Edmund H. Sears

Chapter One

November, 1862

Rain pelted down on Ephraim, rolling off the brim of his hat and streaming onto his jacket. He pulled the wool collar closer around his neck and lowered his head to shield his face. What had started as a mist was now turning to a steady rain. And if he knew the Virginia weather, it would soon become a downpour. His meager layer of clothing would be no match for the storm's fury.

Shenandoah nickered softly and stamped her hooves. Ephraim patted her neck, sympathetic to her impatience. He knew the feeling well.

The moon had only just peeked through the low branches of the trees when he had arrived at the old oak that constituted their meeting place. It had now risen high above, judging by the clouds' faint, eerie glow.

Something wasn't right. His contact would've been there long ago unless there was trouble.

He would wait only a short while longer before abandoning the meeting. It was growing more evident as each second passed that no one was going to appear.

The longer he spent in one place only increased the chances of trouble.

He dismounted, boots sinking into a layer of mud. His hand brushed the bark of the old oak. Were his fingers not cold and wet from the storm, he would have keenly felt the ridges and grooves that characterized the tree. Its ashen color blended into the surroundings of moonlight and mist.

There was security in its branches and boughs, so familiar to a native Virginian. Tall and proud these mighty white oaks stood, witnesses to hundreds of years gone by. Of the first Virginians to settle in the mountains and valleys, of the Indian wars, and the birth of a fledgling nation. Centurions in their own right, they stood as guardians of the land now threatened by the foot of an invader.

He ran his hand over the surface, searching for the slightly raised portion that served as a hatch to the hollow space inside. One sweep of the tree uncovered nothing. He was certain this was the correct side. Maybe the hollow was lower than he remembered.

His eyes strained in the darkness. Another sweep of the bark. This time his hand caught the edge of the hatch. It swung sideways to reveal the small hollow.

If his contact had left a message or parcel for him, it would be in the hollow. A thorough search assured him that none had been left.

Tension clenched his body. Any number of things could've happened. But of one thing he was absolutely sure — it couldn't be good.

He settled into Shenandoah's saddle. "Let's get out of here, huh?"

She moved forward obediently. He steeled himself against the driving rain. It wouldn't be much longer before the weather turned and tiny flakes of snow would come down in place of the rain. There was once a time when the promise of snow would have caused excitement to well inside him. But that had changed. It brought back too many memories he wished would die. Each snowflake was a grain of salt poured on the wound of his soul.

Winter made him long for the spring thaw to melt away the sorrows that haunted him, though they never truly were put to rest. That would take a miracle he was quite certain would never come.

Shenandoah moved with ease through the trails leading them back to camp. He half expected to run into a Yankee picket. But, evidently, even the Yanks had no desire to be out in the kind of weather the night held. Trees and shrubs passed silently until the familiar landmarks came to view assuring him he had made it safely to camp.

Ordinarily, he would breathe a bit easier, but the unexplained absence of his contact bothered him. Taylor knew the importance of his role in aiding the scouts. It wasn't like him to not show up.

Ephraim pulled back the reins gently, slowing Shenandoah as they approached the outskirts of camp.

"Who goes there?" A burly voice resonated from the inky shadows.

"Sergeant Bryant. As if you didn't know." Ephraim leaned forward in his saddle, impatiently waiting for the source of the voice to appear. It was a necessary annoyance to go through the checkpoint before entering camp, even if the picket could see that it was another of the scouts.

"Well now, who's to say you aren't a Yankee spy *pretending* to be Sergeant Bryant?" Christian MacCammon emerged from the darkness concealing him. Rifle in hand, he sauntered forward with a mischievous grin that carried all the way to his eyes. "All I see is a coat as blue as General Burnside's himself."

Ephraim glanced down at the Federal coat he wore over his Confederate uniform to conceal his allegiance during his excursions in enemy territory. "Come on, Chris. Quit messing around. I'm cold and sopping wet. Besides that, I need to talk to the captain."

Chris allowed his teasing to fade away at the soberness in Ephraim's words. "Bad news?"

"I don't know. I hope not, but I'm not counting on it. No one showed tonight. Not a package, not a note, nothing." Ephraim shook his head. "It's not like him."

A gust of wind howled in the tree branches above them.

Ephraim braced against the shiver that ran down his spine.

"Sir, I need to find out what happened. His last letter said he would have more information on troop movements in the area at our next meeting." Ephraim perched on the edge of the makeshift cot belonging to his commander. The wind pressed against the sides of the canvas tent, threatening to bring it down around them. He was still miserably wet, but it could be worse.

Captain Flanagan rubbed his face, pacing to the tent entrance then back again. In absence of the worn, dusty cap he typically wore, russet peaks of hair stood in disheveled mutiny. Semi-permanent furrows remained where he had raked his fingers a thousand times over the last few months.

War weighed heavy on a man's shoulders. Giving orders that determined the life or death of young men in his command weighed even heavier on the namesake of Flanagan's Scouts. Deep creases carved grooves in his forehead and at the corners of his eyes.

"Aye, and if something's gone wrong, the Yanks might be waiting for you."

Ephraim gripped the brim of his hat tightly. "But they might not be, sir. With all respect, I don't think there is much choice."

Flanagan turned abruptly, staring at Ephraim through steely eyes. "And if you're wrong, you'll find yourself the guest of honor at a lynching party." He dropped his gaze, jaw clenched. "That's one party I'd just as soon you not attend."

Ephraim bit the inside of his lip. It was better to let Flanagan ponder his request, think about how important this was. Though the captain had inherited his Irish ancestors' fiery temper and disposition, he wasn't one to make hasty judgments. Ephraim supposed that was a necessary quality when commanding a force of men.

"All right. Take MacCammon with you. You'll be wise to make use of the rain while you have it. It'll wash away any tracks."

Ephraim was on his feet before Captain Flanagan was mid-sentence. He snapped a salute. "Yessir."

Now to break the news to Chris.

He found him by the pitiful remains of the fire, which was fighting to keep aglow. "Don't get too used to warmth just yet. You and I have some reconnaissance to do."

Chris heaved a sigh. "Now?"

Ephraim nodded and checked the girth of his saddle once again. "For once the weather is working in our favor."

Chris groaned and left to ready his mount. Ephraim patted Shenandoah, and pulled a small hand of grain from her saddlebag. "Just one more ride tonight, girl. I want to bed down just as bad as you."

"MacCammon is saddling up. Where are you going?"

Ephraim recognized the young voice to belong to the scouts' youngest member. He finished feeding the grain and brushed his hand on his pant leg. "On a mission."

By the glow of the firelight he could see the boy's eyes glimmer with excitement. "Can I go with you this time? Chris told me that I could go with you some time."

Of course he did.

Ephraim pulled himself into the saddle as Chris rode toward him. "I don't know what MacCammon told you, but we don't need you tonight."

A stab of guilt pricked his heart as the boy's face fell in disappointment.

So much like Sam.

"Remy! Let me go with you. Please!"

"You can't this time, but someday I'll take you and show you everything. I promise."

He quickly brushed aside the painful memory. War was not a game or an adventure. It was raw, real, and unfair, just like life. The sooner Gideon learned that fact would be for the better. He watched Gideon's form melt into the darkness surrounding camp.

"You know, you don't have to be so harsh on him. He thinks the world of you," Chris murmured.

Ephraim straightened and nudged Shenandoah forward. "You need to stop encouraging him, Chris. You shouldn't have told him that he could go with us. What were you thinking? He doesn't know the first thing about the realities of this war. And to be frank, I have more things on my mind than playing nursemaid to him."

Chris' silence told Ephraim that judgement had already been passed on the situation. That was just fine. Chris could pass judgement from where he sat, but he wasn't Ephraim and he never would be.

"Tell me I'm wrong," he said.

"You're wrong."

The hasty retort caused Ephraim to clench his jaw. Chris had grown to become a trusted friend. But at times he was insufferable.

"He looks up to you, Ephraim," Chris said. "You're the scout he wants to be. I would think you'd be honored."

"I don't want him to look up to me," Ephraim snapped. "Is that so hard to understand? I've been there and done that. I'm not wanting for his admiration or company. He'd do better to learn that no one is worth the pain that comes from forming relationships. No one."

The coals of the past kindled again into a blaze of anger. He thought they had finally begun to extinguish, that perhaps he would be able to leave them far behind. Clearly he was wrong. They burned hotter now than they had before.

The expression on Chris' face was one of hesitant shock. He stammered slightly in search of a response, then stopped altogether. Ephraim bristled against the gnawing emotions that ate away at him. Why should he feel remorse for his words? Chris was the one who hadn't left well enough alone.

Besides, it wasn't being harsh to admit that he had no desire to foster any sort of admiration from the kid. It was better for both of them if he stamped it out before it got a chance to begin.

They rode in silence for a time, tension evident between them. Ephraim figured the quiet would give their tempers time to cool. Eventually, he knew the tension would break and they would go on as usual.

Hopefully Chris would take the hint that the discussion was over.

"To think I could be back at camp sound asleep by now," Chris muttered finally. "The Bluedevils just can't let a man be." Though the topic had changed, it was evident that the demeanor of both men had not.

Ephraim shifted in his saddle, voice grim. "If they did, we wouldn't be here in the first place."

Shenandoah picked her way carefully through the brush and shrubs that constituted the trail. Ephraim tilted his head back, eyes fixed on the shadowy clouds that covered the moon now.

Lord, I'd be mighty grateful if you'd keep the rain coming down. Just until we're back to camp for the night.

"Glory, how I wish they *would*." Chris interrupted his thoughts, returning to the topic of the Federals. "I'd be home with a cup of the strongest coffee this side of the Blue Ridge, a crackling fire, and a slice of Peg's pecan cake. Not to mention a real bed." He sighed, his eyes exuding homesickness.

Ephraim shook his head. The MacCammon name meant Chris had been born into upper society — rarely, if ever, wanting for anything in his twenty years. Occasionally, Ephraim wondered what it would be like to come from such a family, but he figured it wasn't worth it after seeing how much the boys put Chris through the mill for it. Most of the scouts came from homes like Ephraim, living hand to mouth. Their paths would've never crossed with someone with the MacCammon status, much less eat and sleep together like the scouts did. War was odd that way. It took the unheard of and made it plausible.

Through the hazy darkness the silhouette of the old oak emerged. They were in the Blue Bellies' backyard now. He glanced to the side, catching Chris' eyes.

Chris nodded and nudged his mount forward to keep pace with Shenandoah. They rode in perfect silence for near fifteen minutes, taking note of every noise or anything that seemed out of place.

A short while more would bring them to the Taylor farm, where Ephraim hoped to find his contact unscathed and unharmed. It would be helpful if he was also able to inform them of what was happening. There had been an unusual amount of Yankee activity of late.

Ephraim pulled up on his reins. Chris had come to a stop, gaze combing every inch of the darkness. He signaled to Ephraim that he heard something. They looped around behind the cover of a pine tree, watching the trail they had just come from for any sign of trouble.

Ephraim squinted into the night, then nudged Chris. He gestured toward the shadowed figure on horseback now emerging from where they had come. The figure rode at a steady pace, as though trying to overtake them. Ephraim grit his teeth and leaned forward. He didn't like the feeling he was getting. He looked to Chris and sucked in a deep breath. It was evident that Chris shared his hunch.

Of all the fool things that boy could've done.

They waited until the rider was nearly to them, then spurred their mounts onto the trail to cut him off.

The rider pulled back hard on his reins to avoid colliding with them and nearly slid from his saddle. Ephraim reached, and seized the reins from him. "What are you doing?" he hissed, trying to keep his voice from rising to a shout.

Gideon stammered and sputtered in search of an answer. Ephraim didn't give him the time to find one before going on. "Do you realize that we might have been a Yankee picket? And you would now be our prisoner to do with as we please. Are you mad?" He turned to Chris. "Take him back to camp. I'll meet you back there."

Gideon started to protest but shrank back when Ephraim gave him a glaring look. Then, from behind the curtain of ink that shrouded the woods, a branch snapped. A voice called out for them to halt and dismount. Adrenaline surged through Ephraim and he slapped the flank of Gideon's horse, sending it forward into the night. Ephraim spurred Shenandoah into a full gallop. A shot cracked through the air. Pain ripped through his arm with a fierce burning. Then another shout and the hurried shuffle of others joining the lone picket.

The Yanks knew they were present now. No telling how much time they could gain before a full posse was gathered to come after them.

Thank the Almighty for the rain. We just might have a chance of getting out alive.

Mariah hugged her shawl tight against her body. The night held a haunting uneasiness that she couldn't quite place. Papa's arrest had brought a dark cloud over the house. It blocked out the brightness and threatened to shake the household to its very core. It was no wonder an unsettling aura lingered. Mother had been called to the Branfield home to aid in the birth of their third child. It wasn't unusual for Papa and Mama both to be gone for a time, leaving the house and Benjamin in Mariah's care. Such was the life of a pastor and his family. The war had only added to that burden. And it *was* a burden, though Papa would rarely admit it. It had only gotten worse in the short month since the Yankees arrived.

But tonight was different. Papa wouldn't be riding up the path any time now, sending a blessed security through the household. No...tonight held a sense of foreboding that she couldn't shake away. Supper had finished long ago and the dishes were cleaned and put away. After reading aloud for a time, she had sent Benjamin to bed. She should've followed. But it was useless to try sleeping while her mind teetered on the edge of so much uncertainty.

"'Peace I leave with you, my peace I give unto you: not as the world giveth, give I unto you. Let not your heart be troubled, neither let it be afraid.'"

She quoted the familiar verse aloud, hoping it would magically erase the anxiety sweeping through her. But it didn't. It only added to the confusion.

How could there be peace when their world lay in ruins around them? Her heart *was* troubled, and there seemed no remedy no matter how hard she tried.

She pulled back the curtain that covered the window overlooking the yard. Had she remembered to secure the barn door after finishing her work? A rash of thefts and looting had accompanied the arrival of federal troops. It wouldn't hurt to make sure everything was secure for the night.

She winced against the wind that sliced her with its daggers as she stepped onto the porch. Fat raindrops splashed down from the inkwell of blackness covering the sky. The night was cooler than she had expected. She would give Tempest an extra fork of straw. Her footsteps made soft pattering sounds against the muddy ground as she hurried to find shelter within the walls of the old barn.

The door groaned as she slid it open. She stopped just inside. Were her eyes playing tricks on her or had something moved in the far corner? Tempest whinnied as though unsettled. Mariah turned to quiet her, ignoring the gooseflesh now covering her own arms.

An airy sound, as though someone were laboring to draw breath, sent Mariah's heart racing. She and Tempest weren't alone in the barn. Cautiously she backed toward the door. But it was too late.

Shadowy figures appeared before her like ghosts in the night. Two in front of her and one approaching from the side. The foggy darkness added to the chilling sight.

A scream — her own — echoed into the night.

"No, please," one figure pleaded in a hoarse whisper. "We mean no harm."

Mariah felt behind her for anything that could be a weapon if she needed it to be. Her hand found the handle of the hay fork. She thrust it forward between herself and the men.

"Whoah, easy, miss," one said.

A voice broke the stillness, this one some distance away outside. "They can't have gone far. Circle around and see what you can find."

She could now see more clearly the faces of the figures. Two of them seemed close to her own age. The third was little more than a child. All of them had panic written on their faces. Blood oozed from the arm of the one who stood near the child. The sounds of voices growing louder spurred them into action.

The wounded one grabbed her by the arm and pulled her toward the door. "We don't have time. To the house," he urged.

"What are you doing? Let go of me," Mariah hissed. Confusion clouded the situation. Who were these men, and why were they roaming around the farm in the middle of the night? More importantly, who were they hiding from?

There wasn't time for the questions to form on her tongue, much less get answers to them. They clambered up the steps leading to the house. The door closed softly behind them.

Chapter Two

The man with the bleeding arm leaned against the window. "If they come to the house, tell them you haven't seen us."

Mariah opened her mouth to protest, but the mysterious trio were already ducking into the adjoining room. She followed, stopping just shy of the doorway. "Who are you? You can't just barge into someone's home and expect them to help you."

"We're friends of your father's. We'll tell you more later. But for now will you just trust us? You'll be doing your country a favor."

"What do you know of my father?" She eyed them suspiciously. Her hand felt the smooth knob of Papa's desk drawer behind her. It harbored his revolver. She would use it if she had to. "And why should I trust you? For all I know, you're Bluecoats."

At this the wounded one cocked his head with frustration, gripping his bloodied arm with a wince. "Do you think I'd have this if we were? Or that we would be in danger of getting lynched by that mob out there?"

Mariah huffed. "With the manners you possess, it wouldn't surprise me."

He opened his mouth as if to offer a retort, but a pounding echoed from the door and they all went silent.

"You inside the house, open up!"

"Quickly," she hissed, motioning for them to follow her. At the back of the room she smoothed her hand along the wood paneling until she felt a small crack. When pulled back, a small room was revealed. The men took refuge inside without a word and she returned the faulty panel to its place.

Another shouted command to open the door came from outside. She practically sprinted to the desk, pulling the revolver from its place in the drawer and concealing it beneath her shawl. Then made her way to the door. Her hand trembled as it closed around the brass doorknob. A nightmare could not have been more unreal or unsettling.

She opened it only part way to see into the night. The porch was occupied by a half dozen soldiers of the Union. Their leader stood nearest the door, hand resting upon his sword. She knew him. Captain Jacob Amsden.

Mariah met his gaze, not offering a word. It was difficult to find anything cordial to say to the man who was responsible for her father's arrest.

He stepped closer to the opening. "Are you alone in the house?"

"Of course not. My family is here with me." She prayed her voice didn't betray her. It wasn't a lie, after all. Benjamin was sleeping upstairs — or he *had* been.

He gazed beyond her into the house. Mariah closed the opening so that he could see as little as possible. The fact that these Yankee invaders thought they could have free reign of the civilian homes and farms made her burn with fury.

"It's been reported that three riders passed through here in the last quarter of an hour. Most likely Reb scouts. Have you seen anyone?"

"Sir, it's late. How on earth would I have seen these alleged riders in the dead of night from within my house?"

He narrowed his eyes. "One of my men said they heard a woman scream a short time ago."

Mariah raised an eyebrow. "Then I suggest you go look for a woman who lacks the presence of mind to know better than to be roaming these woods at night, instead of one who is trying to keep her young sibling from being awakened by your pounding on our door."

A glare met her response. The man opened his mouth, but was cut short when a soldier came running up. "Captain, sir. There is no one in the barn or immediate area."

Amsden steeled his face, sucked in a breath, and nodded his acknowledgement to the soldier. Another glance back to Mariah, his gaze moving beyond her to what he could see of the room. "I'm afraid I'm going to have to insist on checking inside."

Mariah stepped back, clearing a path for the soldiers to enter. "You really haven't anything better to do?"

They trampled in with the noise of a stampede. Indeed, a stampede might have been quieter. It wasn't long before Benjamin clambered down the stairs, wide-eyed and alert to the invasion of his home. Mariah motioned for him to stand behind her, out of the way of the soldiers. Amsden hardly seemed satisfied when every room turned up empty of any rebel scouts. But he couldn't argue with his own eyes.

He stormed out the door, muttering an apology for disturbing her. She breathed a silent sigh of relief as the men followed their leader down the steps and into the night. She wasted no time closing and bolting the door. From the window she watched as they disappeared down the road.

"What's going on? Why did they come," Benjamin asked, now wide awake.

Mariah collected her composure and laid her hand on his shoulder. "Nothing for you to worry about. Now back to bed, before Mama returns and finds you up."

Reluctantly, he disappeared up the stairs. Mariah released a breath. Now to deal with the other issue at hand — the fugitives she had just risked everything for.

Her skirts swished around her ankles as she spun toward the men emerging from their hiding place. "They're gone," she said.

"Much obliged. Your country is indebted to you," the well-mannered one said. He bowed. "Corporal MacCammon at your service, miss."

Mariah nodded with a leery gaze. Her hand still tightly gripped the revolver. They didn't seem to be interested in causing trouble. But then again, they *had* barged into her home uninvited. The two older soldiers were armed with revolvers. Additionally, a sword hung at the side of the one who was wounded. He had returned to the window and drew back the curtain. A wince crossed his face with the movement of his injured arm. "We're looking for Ezekiel Taylor. You're his daughter, I assume?"

Corporal MacCammon moved toward his friend, cocking his head to examine the wound. "Do you have something to dress this with?"

"You may as well sit down," Mariah stated. "It'll need to be cleaned first."

It took only a short time to gather what supplies could be found in the house. Most had been used to help the wounded before the Yankees had come.

MacCammon had seated his friend and removed the dark coat, revealing Confederate gray. Relief washed over Mariah at the sight of the familiar uniform. They were beginning to look less like a threat, especially being as they had a child with them.

A splotch of crimson bled through the hole that now pocked the wool coat and shirt beneath. MacCammon peeled back the layers of fabric and poured a dipper of water over the wound. His friend drew back reflexively.

"Hold still, Bryant."

Mariah held back a cringe and returned her thoughts to the question asked of her earlier. "My father isn't here. Why are you looking for him?"

Bryant and MacCammon exchanged a look. Bryant spoke for them this time. "We were supposed to meet him tonight."

"With regard to his ... work?"

They exchanged another glance that Mariah couldn't miss. "Yes."

MacCammon looked up from his work. "Do you have any honey?"

Bryant started to stand up in protest. "Just hold on a minute. What are you fixing to do?"

MacCammon pushed him back down. "Don't get your dander up. My grandmother used to use it on me whenever I got a cut. Best remedy there is."

From the expression on Bryant's face, he was still leery of the idea. Mariah opened the small cabinet nearest the fireplace. Tucked away behind the jars and bottles containing spices and grains stood a small pot of honey, gathered in the summer. She offered it to MacCammon, who took a small amount and slathered it on the bloodied flesh. Mariah looked away. She had helped with the work many times when the hogs were ready to butcher, and the blood had never bothered her. But it was a sight different when the blood belonged to a human being.

"Do you know what he had for us?"

Mariah furrowed her brow. "You were expecting the Bibles, weren't you?"

Now it was Bryant's turn to be confused. He cocked his head slightly and started to speak, but the color drained from his face as MacCammon continued doctoring. He squeezed his eyes shut to block it out.

"We don't know anything about any Bibles, miss," MacCammon stated. "Taylor was supposed to be — giving us some insight into the area."

Silent up until now, the boy with them perked up. His eyes gleamed with intrigue. "You mean a spy?"

Mariah flashed her gaze back to MacCammon and Bryant, searching their faces. Something told her they were not discussing the same thing.

Bryant cringed, and sucked in a deep breath. "Chris," he muttered, a hint of anger mingling with annoyance.

MacCammon looked knowingly at the boy. He was apparently the go-between in the trio.

"I know. I know. I've already caused enough problems," the boy said, defeatedly shrinking back into the corner of the room.

MacCammon nodded. "Don't you think you better just sit quietly?"

"I take it you aren't aware of your father's dealings. Have you heard of Flanagan's Scouts?" Bryant spoke through clenched teeth. Beads of perspiration gathered around his temples in spite of the cool air.

"Who in these parts hasn't?"

The scouts were loved by the people. They had become a sort of legend, as if their missions against the Yankees were comparable to Robin Hood's escapades in Sherwood Forest.

"Flattered that our reputation precedes us," MacCammon said. He flashed a jaunty grin. A sparkle gleamed in his eyes.

Bryant cleared his throat, silencing his companion with only a look. "Your father has been an integral part of aiding us in our intelligence operations. We were supposed to meet tonight, but he never showed up."

The words took a moment to fully compute in Mariah's mind. This went beyond smuggling Bibles. These rogue men were Flanagan Scouts? It was no wonder the Yankees were out for blood. And Papa...how long had he been involved in spying? She had known of the efforts to smuggle Bibles into Confederate territory. But spying?

Bryant cocked his head. "Maybe you should sit down, Miss Taylor. You...look pale."

Heat flushed Mariah's face. "This coming from the man who appears he's seen a haint."

MacCammon elbowed Bryant. "What he means is, it's understandable that you might be caught off guard by this information."

From the short time Mariah had known the two men it seemed Sergeant Bryant would do good to learn a few manners from MacCammon.

"You don't know then," she said, sinking into the chair across from them.

Their expressions were answer enough. Mariah willed herself to speak the words that stung so much. "He was arrested day before last by the Yankees. Contraband charges for attempting to carry Bibles across lines."

Sergeant Bryant clenched his fist, clearly fighting to keep from slamming it down on the table. He pinched the bridge of his nose, eyes closed, silent.

MacCammon paused his work winding the strip of cloth around the bleeding wound.

Finally, Bryant spoke. "And now we don't know what information he had for us." They remained quiet for a moment. Then Bryant spoke again. "Do you know where they took him?"

"He's being held in the county jail until his trial."

"If they give him a trial," Bryant murmured more to himself than anyone.

MacCammon coughed, once again reminding his sergeant to keep manners.

"Thank you for your kindness, Corporal MacCammon, but there's no need to spare me. I'm aware of what the Yankees are capable of."

"We've got to find out what he knows." Bryant studied the grain of the table, undoubtedly not hearing a word of the conversation going on around him.

Flames of indignity kindled deep inside Mariah's spirit. Was that all he thought of? What of her father, the man who had sacrificed his freedom for them in the first place?

"You'll just let him remain at their mercy then?" The words formed in an accusatory tone before she could stop them.

If nothing else, it seemed to pull him from the depths of his thoughts. He lifted his gaze to meet hers. "That's not my decision to make, Miss Taylor. The information he carried could be a matter of life or death for a lot of our boys, though. And that *is* my problem."

"And how do you propose we go about accomplishing that?" MacCammon tied off the bandage. He looked with disdain on his hands, now covered in blood, then down at his well kept clothing as though pondering what he should do about it. "Here. I think this belongs to you," he said, wiping the crimson substance on Bryant's uniform.

"Thanks," Bryant grumbled. He eased his arm back into his coat sleeve.

"You didn't answer my question. We can't just stride in and demand they hand him over to us. Least ways not unless we want our necks stretched."

Mariah felt the gaze of Sergeant Bryant rest on her. She shifted her eyes up. Why was he looking at *her*?

"I know it would be asking a lot, Miss Taylor. But you seem to be our only chance."

Her heart beat against her ribs. "Me? And how do you propose I do it?"

"You know where they are holding your father. You could easily pass off your presence as an attempt to visit him," MacCammon responded.

"He'll know what to do when you mention us. But you can't let anyone hear you. We can hope that the Yankees have no inkling that he was working with us in this manner. His chance of living is much higher if they only believe him to be involved in the smuggling of Bibles."

Fear and overwhelm fought for control of Mariah's mind. What would happen if she was caught? The consequences of such an action was not lessened with the fact that she was a woman.

"You can't be serious," she said.

Bryant raised an eyebrow. "We *are* serious, Miss Taylor. You would be helping your country immensely."

Mariah smoothed her hand over the apron covering her skirt. This was madness. Smuggling had landed Papa in prison. How could they expect her to now willingly risk the same fate? If it was true that the Yankees weren't aware of his involvement with the scouts, why would she risk drawing it to their attention?

She shook her head. "I'm sorry. You'll have to find some other way."

Sergeant Bryant shared a look with McCammon. "Miss, it is of the utmost importance that—"

"You'll have to find someone else," she repeated with emphasis.

Tension crept up Bryant's jawline and into his temples. He stood, McCammon and the boy following suit, and walked to the door. There he stopped and looked at her again. "Would you not at least try it?"

When would he realize that her final answer was no? She loved the Confederacy. But she loved Papa more.

"We've lost enough, Sergeant. How much more do you require from us?"

"Many have, miss. It's a sad state, but you're not the only family that has suffered at the hand of war." His eyes flashed with indignation. "Forgive me for thinking that surely the daughter of a man like Ezekiel Taylor would be able to see past her own needs for a greater cause. I was wrong, I can see."

He stormed out the door and mounted alongside his friends. Mariah placed her hands on her hips.

Good riddance.

Fumes built inside her. That man was insufferable. His temper was almost as bad as his manners. He had no room to judge her. This war had stolen enough from her without asking for this now.

Chapter Three

They had found the horses where they had left them a distance from the Taylor farm and had finally arrived back to camp, soaked to the skin and longing for sleep. Ephraim sent Gideon to bed down with the promise that they would be speaking with Captain Flanagan about his actions come morning.

"'*You look pale, maybe you should sit down*?'" Chris raised an eyebrow, questioning Ephraim's choice of words.

"What was wrong with that? She *did* look pale. The last thing I needed was to have her crumple to the floor in front of me."

Chris cringed and shook his head. "With your manners, or lack thereof, it's no wonder she wouldn't agree to our plan."

"Hmph." Ephraim loosened the girth of his saddle and slid it from Shenandoah's back. Fire burned through his arm. "She looked apt to shoot us."

"Can you blame her? You practically told her that your only concern was getting the intelligence he had gathered for us."

A bone-deep weariness settled over Ephraim. Back to the relative safety of their own territory. Back to the secure comfort of camp. Were he not seeing double and swaying in his steps from the lack of sleep, he may have had an answer for Chris. But, as it stood, the only thing on his mind was catching a few hours of sleep before the sun crept above the skyline. After that, Chris could rebuke him for all manner of things he had done wrong. Appalling manners, stating the obvious when no one else would, keeping his mind focused solely on their job. He wouldn't really care once he had some sleep.

What was he supposed to do anyway? Tell her the scouts would break her father out of prison and all would be well like something from a child's tale? Life didn't work that way and neither did war.

Would Captain Flanagan try to free Ezekiel Taylor? It was quite probable. Taylor was a tremendous aid in the gathering of intelligence in and around his county, and a brave citizen of the Confederacy. It wasn't likely Flanagan would sit by idly and see a man unjustly punished for being a God-fearing patriot. But there were times when the good of the cause had to be placed at a higher priority than one individual. That rang true in this situation.

Chris arched his back and rubbed his neck. "Apart from almost being impaled by Miss Taylor's pitchfork, tonight was a little too close for comfort if you ask me. I don't know why I ever signed up for this."

Ephraim hid a smirk. Chris grumbled a lot on the outside, but he was a good soldier deep down.

He sank to the ground atop the blanket shielding him from the mud. Chris joined him. A few minutes passed with nothing but the sounds of the crackling fire fighting to keep alive against the wind.

"I wouldn't care to have to hide there again," Chris said. "But I reckon we weren't the first ones to hide for our lives there."

Ephraim nodded. It didn't surprise him that Chris had guessed the secret room's purpose. Hidden places had hidden purposes. When paired with the outspoken views of the Taylor family, it was easy enough to piece together why the room existed.

The topic had never come up between Pastor Taylor and Ephraim in the time they had known each other, but it didn't surprise him. Many preachers were involved in the clandestine operations of the Underground Railway. Ezekiel Taylor was the type of man to be one of them. He based his life on the Scriptures and if something didn't line up with them, it had to be changed. Slavery was one such evil.

For a time only the ghostly wind spoke as it moaned and whistled through the limbs and branches. Then, finally, sleep settled over them.

Mama brushed back a wisp of hair that had fallen free over her forehead. In its wake a stripe of flour remained. She tugged on a corner of the dough she was kneading and folded it into the middle, pushing it down again.

"It was safer for you not to know."

Mariah looked up from the simmering pot she stirred. Her mind reeled with the information brought to light from the previous night. She had known about the smuggling. Occasionally, Papa had even sent her to carry a small shipment across lines. But Bible smuggling was a sight different than spying. If the federals found out, Papa would hang. It was one more burden added to the unbearable weight they already carried.

She dropped a sprinkle of herbs into the boiling broth, savoring the delicious aroma it created. "Do you think they know?"

Mama sighed and paused, her hands still pressing firmly into the dough. "I don't know. If they do, we'll need a miracle to see him released."

Mariah bit the inside of her cheek. It bothered her that she was unable to do anything to help any of the situations she found herself to be privy to. A nagging drive to fix the issues at hand echoed through her.

She was never much for patience, though it wasn't for lack of Mama and Papa's teaching. It seemed to be a recurring theme as a child. Clearly, not much had taken root.

She brought a hand to her temples, trying her best to rub away the worry. "What if they do know? What if they hang him?"

The words were out before she could process them. Hearing her thoughts out loud only encouraged her heart to race faster. Suddenly a dozen more thoughts welled up.

What if they never got a chance to see him again? What if God let him die? How would they survive the unthinkable?

Mama rested her hands on the table's edge, gaze fixed on Mariah. "The what-ifs of tomorrow are not for us to carry today," she said firmly. "The Almighty is still in control, and we are not going to entertain thoughts otherwise."

Sometimes it drove her mad, how calm Mama managed to be regardless of the situation. Mariah believed God was in control, but it still didn't ease the questions of tomorrow.

She took a breath and slowly released it. "What do you think Papa was going to tell them?"

For all they knew it could be a matter of urgency for the army. And yet, there in the county jail, the secret remained with him.

Mama lifted the dough and patted it, then placed it on the pan for baking. "Likely something to do with the sudden influx of troops in the area. But what it all means ..."

Wild squeals filled the air, drawing Mariah's attention. Something had the hogs riled up. She rested the ladle on the table and brushed her hands on the apron covering her skirt.

Before she reached the door, it swung open and Benjamin burst through. His face was white and his eyes wide. "Yankees, Mama. Yankees in the barn."

Her heart skipped a beat, then started pounding so hard she thought for sure it would give out. Benjamin stepped to the side of the doorway. In the yard, a troop of Bluejackets swarmed. The barn doors were wide open and soldiers were carrying out armfuls of goods.

Mariah's mouth went dry. Hidden beneath the old floorboards, scattered with straw and dust, remained the other half of the Bibles awaiting their journey to Confederate lines. Could they be the reason for this raid? Had Amsden sent them to search for more contraband to ensure Papa's sentence was long and hard?

One soldier carried three hens, their necks having already been wrung. Another carried a sack of feed.

Benjamin looked with fury at the sight. "Mama, they're stealing them!"

Mama laid her hand on his shoulder. "Stay still, Benjamin. I would rather lose a few chickens than a son."

Sweat slicked Mariah's hands. They could survive the loss of the chickens. But if the Bibles were found...

Three soldiers approached the porch. Their uniforms were dusty, and an odor came off them like Mariah hadn't smelt before. They carried rifles over their shoulders — a poignant reminder that they were in charge.

The one who seemed in charge growled at Mama. "Where is your food store?"

"If you and your men are hungry, you need only to ask. I have never turned away a hungry soul from my table."

Mariah didn't know how Mama could be so gracious to men who were so revolting. If it was left to her, she could think of a few stinging words to share with them.

He grinned with a smile, missing teeth. "I don't need to ask for nothing from you Rebs."

The two soldiers with him pushed their way past, practically knocking Benjamin out of the way. Mariah tried to calm the steadily rising fear inside her. Tales of these rogue Yankee bands had made their way all over Virginia. Thievery, ransacking, and other unspeakable crimes were most often the result. They had even heard of a man being hanged to death in his own front yard by a band of Yankees. A shiver worked its way down her spine. Mama slipped her arm into the crook of Mariah's elbow, as if she knew her fear.

Lord, preserve us.

One of the soldiers had found Mama's porcelain plates and was smashing them against the fireplace. The delicate plates shattered into thousands of tiny fragments that would never be able to be restored. Another rifled through the cupboards, taking anything that suited him.

The one who had spoken to them made his way up the porch steps and stopped before them. His rifle was leveled at Mama, sunlight glinting off the bayonet.

"Where's your money?"

They stood silently.

"Are you deaf, woman?" The soldier narrowed his eyes at Mama, then swung his rifle toward Benjamin. "Your son could easily become a casualty of war."

Mariah stifled a gasp. She clenched her hands around the fabric of her skirt.

Mama maintained her stoic expression. She stepped into the doorway and retrieved the small wooden box that held their meager income. "Here is all the money I have."

He took it and greedily threw back the lid. He paused for a moment as he gazed into the box. "Reb money," he spat. "Nothing but worthless Reb money."

With a curse, he threw the box and its contents to the ground. Mariah winced at the smashing sound as it collided with the floor. She watched from the corner of her eye to see what the soldier would do. His face had gone red and his eyes burned with fury. He kicked the box across the floor with all his might. It slammed into the wall and splintered down the center. With another angry shout, he turned to join his men in their manic plundering.

It was all Mariah could do to tame the fear that threatened to overwhelm her. Benjamin's face was pale, albeit flushed with anger, and Mama's eyes harbored worry. There wasn't a thing they could do but watch as the unruly soldiers turned their home upside down until nothing remained unscathed.

Only once they had taken all they could carry and disappeared down the road did Mama collapse into one of the chairs around the table. Her head rested in the palms of her hands and Mariah thought she could see her shoulders shake with emotion. Benjamin remained quiet, only glancing to Mariah for reassurance in the situation.

For her own part, Mariah found that the shock and fear was quickly being forced to retreat by a much stronger emotion — anger. This was what God gave them after all they had sacrificed? Wasn't it enough that Papa was in prison for taking the Holy Scriptures to the hands of those who were denied it? Papa always taught them that when they stood for right, God would bless them. Yet he had been standing for right and it had only earned him a place in prison. If he had been home instead, those Yankees wouldn't have been so bold. But he wasn't here. And heaven only knew if he ever would be again.

Mama rose from her chair after a while, retreating to the solitude of the bedroom. She closed the door, likely to keep them from hearing her cry. But it proved futile. Mariah cringed at the muffled sobs coming from the room.

"I wish we had never gotten involved with any of this." Mariah spoke through clenched teeth. Her hands still shook from the jarring experience. "I wish we had left, gone further south like the rest of the congregation did when the Yankees came. At least we would be together, safe and secure."

Benjamin straightened with indignity. "We're not turncoats. Papa said it ain't right, the Yankees invading our home like they've done. Somebody has to stand up to them."

"This isn't a game, Benjamin," she snapped. "What good is it going to do anyone if the Yankees hang him?"

She brushed past him and poured her anger into the task of cleaning the mess left in the soldiers' wake. Shattered glass, broken pottery, torn linens. She stooped to retrieve a piece of the glass. Lightly reflected in it, she could see her face and the anger emanating from it.

Ephraim tipped his tin back and allowed the bitter chicory to flood his taste buds. What he wouldn't give for coffee instead of the endless substitutes. Chicory, sweet potato peels, rye — they were all growing mighty old. But they warmed him some, and that was at least something.

"Sergeant Bryant, sir," a voice called to him.

Ephraim released a sigh and tilted his head toward the heavens. Gideon.

"I'm sorry about what happened. I didn't mean any harm. I just wanted to help."

Ephraim looked beyond him to Captain Flanagan, who had followed the boy. Their eyes met with an understanding knowledge. "There isn't much room in this line of work for 'sorry'. We all could've been killed."

Gideon's head dropped low. For a moment a twinge of sympathy pricked Ephraim, but the burning in his arm soon chased away any rebuke of remorse. "Is that it?"

A nod of reply came from Gideon. Ephraim rested his arm against the fallen tree he sat against. "Well get on, then. Don't you have other duties to attend to?"

The boy shuffled off, barely raising his eyes to see where he was going.

"How is your arm?" Captain Flanagan approached, and eased down to the ground beside him.

"Fine, sir." Truth was, he felt terrible. Being caught in the storm the week prior hadn't benefited his health any.

"Well enough that you feel up to riding for me again?"

Excitement filled Ephraim until he felt he might just burst. The thrill of a mission never went away. "Yessir. Where and when?"

Flanagan grinned. "I reckoned you wouldn't be so cross if you could get back out into things again. It's been like wrestling a bear these last few days keeping you back to camp."

Ephraim pushed off the ground with his good arm, intent on the orders he awaited. Upon Flanagan's orders, he had missed multiple excursions since their meeting with the Federals at the Taylor farm. He was anxious to return to duty.

"We'll leave at dusk. Find McCammon and tell him to be ready."

Ephraim saluted and left. He made short work of finding Chris, and they prepared to leave.

"Do you reckon we'll be in danger of getting killed by a pretty young lass again this time?" Chris asked, his words heavy with jest.

A deep, rumbling cough shook Ephraim's frame before he could answer.

Chris allowed his teasing to fade away and he wrinkled his forehead. "That cough sounds bad."

Ephraim shook his head with a dismissive wave. "It's nothing. Barely notice it."

He checked the straps on Shenandoah's saddle, keeping his back to Chris. One look at his face and Chris would know for sure he was lying. He had an uncanny way of knowing these things about Ephraim.

Truth was, Ephraim had noticed the change too. He had started feeling feverish by mid-afternoon the day before. Since then it had only gotten worse. Burning up one minute and freezing cold the next. His throat felt as though it had been sliced by a bayonet.

He could feel Chris' gaze on him — intense, penetrating, knowing.

"Nothing, huh?" Chris wasn't believing a word he said. "I suppose that's why you look as though you are knocking death's door, begging to be let in?"

Ephraim brushed past him, leading Shenandoah by the reins. He didn't have time to come down with anything. Not now. Not with everything that was going on. The Yanks had been on the move. Every day it seemed there was some new development in the situation that warranted the scouts' attention.

He could hear the steady crunch of Chris' boots behind him. "Is there a reason you're sweating profusely on such a mild day?"

Ephraim's heart quickened with his steps. Chris was looking too closely. There wasn't much he could hide from him.

"And you're wearing two coats like you're cold."

Chris grabbed his arm and stepped in front of him, forcing him to stop walking. Ephraim barely bit back a yelp from the pain of Chris' hand digging into his wound.

Their eyes met with an understanding that they both knew what the other was thinking. Chris lifted his chin slowly.

"Don't say anything about it, Chris," Ephraim said. "Please."

"You think you're going to keep this from Flanagan? He's not stupid. You look terrible," Chris hissed, keeping his voice low enough to keep anyone from hearing. "When was the last time you changed the dressing on your arm?"

Ephraim gingerly touched the arm in question. He had rinsed it and wrapped it with a strip of cloth the day after it happened. But since then it had turned a fiery red and the skin around it was warm to the touch.

"I don't know. I don't have much time to think about that. I can't sit out any more missions."

Chris shook his head. "You're about as stubborn as they come."

Ephraim managed a grin. "That's why I'm a scout."

He side-stepped Chris before he had the chance to argue further. Shenandoah nickered softly, following his lead to where the captain waited.

Chapter Four

The scenes of Virginia were fading into dusty hues and the trees cast long shadows as the trio set out. Captain Flanagan led, not giving much information as to their destination. But it became apparent soon enough. They stopped just shy of the clearing Ephraim recognized from a few nights before. The Taylor farm was still and quiet. A few of the windows glowed with light, indicating someone was still awake. All else assured them no trouble awaited.

They dismounted and secured the horses. Then made their way to the little house. Captain Flanagan rapped on the door. A scuffling sound came from inside. Then a woman's voice. "Who is it?"

"A friend of your husband's, Mrs. Taylor."

The sound of a bolt sliding came, then the door opened a crack.

"I presume your daughter has told you of her meeting with my men a few nights past?"

At this, Mrs. Taylor opened the door enough for them to see her silhouette against the light in the house.

"Captain Flanagan, ma'am," he said with a bow.

McCammon and Ephraim followed their commander's example. Mrs. Taylor stepped to the side and motioned for them to come in.

"I'm sorry to bother you, but we were hoping you could aid us in determining what it is your husband so desperately needed to inform us of."

"It is no bother to be of service to our soldiers, sir." She turned to Mariah, who had come to join them from another room. "But they have denied us the ability to see my husband."

Captain Flanagan ran his hand through his hair as he always did when thinking hard on a subject. His weary eyes met Ephraim's, and he appeared to be contemplating something. He looked again to Mrs. Taylor. "Do you have any medical supplies?"

"Of course," Mrs. Taylor assured. She turned to Mariah briefly. "Fetch what we have from the chest."

Ephraim watched as she left the room. He returned his attention to Flanagan, but realized that both his commander and Mrs. Taylor's gaze were planted solely on his arm. He shifted his weight from one leg to the other.

Mrs. Taylor looked up at him with concern. "When did you change the bandage last?"

Ephraim shrugged. "Not much time to think about that, ma'am."

She shook her head in disapproval. "Well, you do have time now." Her footsteps clicked softly on the floor as she left to see what was keeping Mariah.

Ephraim tilted his head and gazed hard at Chris and Flanagan. "This was hardly fair, sir. If I had known what you were thinking, I wouldn't have come."

Flanagan smirked, a knowing sparkle in his eyes. "I know, lad. That's why I'm a captain and you're not. Don't you think I've noticed the way you cringe anytime something brushes against your arm?"

"I *do not*, sir," Ephraim said.

A sharp pain shot through his arm and shoulder, and he hunched forward, gingerly holding his arm. He looked up to Chris in shock, seasoned with pain. "What was that for?"

"McCammon barely bumped you, and that's your reaction? Aye, son. You're in fine shape." Captain Flanagan patted Ephraim's shoulder. "It won't do us any good if you lose it to the gangrene."

Ephraim shot a glare at Chris. "Thanks a lot," he muttered.

Mrs. Taylor emerged from the other room, her hands full. Setting the supplies on the table, she gently unwrapped the bandage and dabbed away the dried blood while Captain Flanagan continued asking questions regarding Pastor Taylor.

"I'm sure there's no need to tell you of how important your husband has been to our cause." Flanagan leaned forward and spoke with deep passion. "His reconnaissance efforts have proven invaluable. And we've come to rely on him for the supplies we can only come by through compatriots such as your family."

Mrs. Taylor dipped her head slightly in a gracious acknowledgment of his words. "My husband has always believed in duty to one's country."

Captain Flanagan nodded. His boots created heavy thudding sounds as he paced the span of the room. Ephraim was certain he was carefully calculating a plan of some kind.

"The Yanks are planning something. I can feel it," he said. "The area has been buzzing with Bluejackets, like a hornet's nest. So much so that my men have had to lay low and stay out of town completely."

Mariah handed a clean bandage to Mrs. Taylor. "Do you think they're planning an attack?"

"I can't say, miss. But they've got something up their sleeve, that's certain."

Mrs. Taylor paused her work and met Flanagan's gaze. "Sir, my husband is sitting in a Yankee prison for attempting to put the Word of God into the hands of our people. Anything that I can do to oppose the men who would commit such an act, I will happily carry out."

Flanagan rubbed his face thoughtfully. "Anything particular in mind?"

"Our farm sits at the crossroads of town. If the Yankees are planning anything with regard to our lines, they'll have to use that road there or risk getting bogged down in the woodland."

Flanagan's face remained emotionless as he listened. But as Mrs. Taylor concluded her words, a sly grin began to spread. "A fox in the henhouse. What could be better? Bryant, you'll stay. I'll leave Gideon as well in case you need to get word to us quickly."

Ephraim jerked his head up. Stay here? Him? With Gideon? Nothing could've sounded less appealing to him.

Mariah spoke before he could. "But, Mama," she protested, clearly sharing Ephraim's sentiment.

Ephraim stood to register his own complaint. The last thing he wanted was to be stuck with an opinionated woman who already didn't like him and a boy who irritatingly idolized him. "Sir, I'm really not sure I'm the one for the job."

Captain Flanagan turned from the door. "And just who might you be thinking would be?"

"I don't know, sir, but—"

"Then it's settled. You'll stay with them until you hear otherwise from me."

"Good," Mrs. Taylor said. "It'll give you time to heal instead of being out in all manner of weather, succumbing to who-knows-what other types of illness." She placed a motherly hand on his burning forehead and furrowed her brow. "Right now I'm sending you to bed."

Ephraim looked pleadingly at Chris, who shrugged with a sympathetic look. When the captain made up his mind, there was no changing it. That was that. He suppressed a groan. Why him? Why couldn't Chris stay?

Captain Flanagan patted his shoulder as Mrs. Taylor finished winding a strip of clean cloth around his arm. "All for the cause, lad. All for the cause."

"Yessir."

Mrs. Taylor had not been jesting when she ordered Ephraim to bed. He found that out as soon as plans had been settled and Flanagan and Chris left. It was clear that she had commanded a brood of her own children and was not made hesitant in the least by the sergeant's rank he bore. It was no wonder where Mariah had gotten her strong-willed ways.

He had to admit that the chance to rest was one he relished. In their line of work, it had to be taken advantage of whenever the opportunity arose. But two days of doing nothing but lying in bed, coughing and sneezing and choking down the herbal remedies Mrs. Taylor and Mariah concocted, left him nearly stir crazy.

He leaned back against the pillow and breathed a heavy sigh. The soft humming of a woman's voice wafted to him through the door. Then a boy's voice joined. They linked in harmony with one another perfectly. It was reminiscent of home, before everything changed.

He clenched his teeth, eyes flying open. It wasn't bad enough he was miserably bored, but he had to endure this now too. It was a form of torment all its own, for it rekindled memories he wished would die.

The humming continued, until finally Ephraim couldn't stand it. He threw back the blanket covering him and pulled on his boots. It didn't matter that he still felt awful. He couldn't stay in this house a minute longer.

The gazes of Mariah and the boys were keenly felt as he entered the main room, heading for the door. As he walked, he tugged on his coat and grabbed his hat from the peg near the door.

"Where are you going?"

He ignored the question from Mariah. He wanted out of the atmosphere that caused so many bad memories to return. That was the very reason he had joined the scouts — to get away from it all.

"Mama will be fit to be tied," Benjamin piped up.

Ephraim walked to the table and retrieved two candles that sat in the middle. "I'll be back in a while," he said, placing them on the windowsill. "Keep these burning in this window. Only move them if there is trouble."

Mariah's eyes shone with disapproval. "Sergeant, you're not well. You'll catch your death out there."

Ephraim checked to ensure his pistol was in its place beside him. "Miss Taylor, do you ever do anything that involves the slightest bit of courage or risk of any kind?"

Mariah pressed her lips together, the dimple in her cheek showing. He had lit a fire in her eyes that could've been seen from a mile away. It was easy to see that she had inherited her father's fiery soul. But somehow it complimented her much better than Pastor Taylor. It lent itself to her dark hair, neatly pinned up, and eyes the color of the forest after a summer rain. She planted a fist on her hip, and might've responded if he weren't already out of ear shot. The door slammed shut behind him.

Night had fallen heavy over the landscape. He tilted his head up to the sky and breathed a sigh of relief. The cold air would make him pay for this decision later, but he would take his chances with that rather than bear the weight of memories best forgotten.

He clenched his hands around the back of his head. How much longer would he be resigned to this?

God, I can't stay here. I can't. Everything reminds me of them.

Bitterness washed over him in a torrent of pain. Moisture threatened to brim over his eyes. He blinked to hold it back.

I've come to reckon with it. And I've moved on. Why do I have to be reminded of them at every turn? It's not fair of you to add Gideon and the Taylors to the burden I already carry.

Nothing but the chattering of the small woodland animals and insects answered. He wandered to the edge of the woods that nestled the farm securely in their grasp. He found a stump to use for a chair and eased down on it. A jarring cough shot pain through his ribcage and back. He groaned. Could things get worse?

"Do you ever do anything that involves the slightest bit of courage or risk of any kind?"

Ephraim's question lingered in Mariah's mind long into the night. He had eventually returned, face flush and damp with a feverish sweat. After enduring Mama's scolding, he complied with her orders to return to bed. All was long since quiet in the house. Soft snoring sounds drifted from the room where Benjamin and Gideon stayed. Mama, having given up her and Papa's room for Ephraim to use, lay beside her, soundly sleeping.

Mariah gazed into the endless darkness. No matter how hard she tried, her mind would not cease the endless whirling.

Ephraim was one to speak of having courage and risk. It wasn't *his* father who was sitting in prison for having done exactly that. And it was likewise not his family who was risking everything to shelter men the Yankees would give anything to hang.

So then why did the question sting so much? Hadn't they given enough to the cause?

Her thoughts drifted to the Bibles hidden beneath the floorboards of the barn — Bibles that were much sought after in the Confederate states blockaded by the Yankees. She knew that many Confederate soldiers would give nearly anything for a copy of the Scriptures to comfort them in the hardships they faced.

But how would we get them through the lines, Lord? And who would be willing to go, after hearing of Papa's arrest?

She fidgeted uncomfortably. There was no way for the Bibles to make it through, and that was all there was to it. It would be foolish to try.

She forced the thoughts away and fought for the sleep she knew would be sorely missed come morning. The night held more unrest and endless tossing and turning before finally morning's light filtered through the windows.

She slipped from the bed quietly and readied for the day. Closing the door softly behind her, she started down the stairs. No doubt the fire would be only a bed of coals, and she would need to rekindle it to make breakfast.

She stopped on the final step, gaze resting on the figure seated by the fireplace. Flames reached for the chimney, changing from yellow to red, then blue and orange. They outlined the figure in a glowing silhouette.

"You're supposed to be in bed," she said.

Ephraim shot a look over his shoulder, startled by her voice. The surprise soon wore off and his expression returned to its normal sullenness.

"Someone had to keep the fire going," he grumbled, voice raspy with the cold that gripped him.

Mariah studied him for a moment. He confused her. Why would it cross his mind to get up in the middle of the night to stoke the fire for them? Especially when he looked miserably ill.

"No one asked you to, Sergeant. We've somehow managed to survive thus far without you." She was aware that her words harbored a sarcastic tone.

"Miss Taylor, I wish as much as you do that I wasn't here. But unfortunately I am. Let's not make things worse than they already are."

His blunt way of speaking was almost as irritating as his lack of manners.

"Besides," he added, "I wouldn't have to be here at all if you had tried to gather the information from your father, like I had asked you to in the first place."

Indignity welled within her chest. "I don't see you walking into the jail and demanding the answers for yourself," she quipped.

He tilted his head in disbelief, and she understood why. It would be fool hardy for one of the scouts to present themselves at the jail. Not only would they suffer for it, but it would reveal Papa's connection with them.

"I would," he said, "if it weren't for the fact that I'm stuck here by order of Captain Flanagan."

Mariah didn't doubt it. He may be incorrigible, rude, and stubborn but something told her he wasn't much afraid of danger. "For that we can both blame him," she said dryly.

Ephraim looked up from the mesmerizing glow of flames. "People who lack the courage to take action to change their circumstances have no room to cast blame on a man who does."

A searing response lingered on Mariah's tongue, held back only by the Holy Spirit.

Ephraim knew he had lit a fire in Mariah that wasn't likely to quell anytime soon. A person would be daft not to notice. He was learning that she didn't hide her emotions well. But that was no concern of his. He was here for one reason and one reason only. As soon as the Yankees made their next move he would be back in the saddle with the scouts, and all of this would be behind him.

The heat wrapped around him as he added another log to the glowing fire. Old habits were hard to break. He thought this was one that he finally had. But he reckoned it was brought to life again by the familiarity of a home and people he was responsible for protecting. How many years, after Papa's death, had he risen to stoke the fire through the long winter nights to ensure Mama and Sam were warm enough?

He gazed harder into the changing flames, afraid to let his mind take the path it was going. He tried to stop it — change course before it took him to a place he couldn't bear. But it was too late.

"I'm cold." The whisper came in the darkness. In the dim light of the fire Ephraim could see Sam's silhouette.

"You should be in bed," Ephraim whispered.

The boy wandered sleepily toward the fireplace, aglow with warmth. He burrowed into the secure shelter of Ephraim's arm and yawned. "I wish I could go with you, Remy."

"I won't be gone forever," he soothed. "And when I come back we'll have the best times together."

A shower of sparks ascended into the chimney as a log shifted and collapsed. It was enough to draw him from his thoughts, but not enough to stamp out the grief that welled.

He rose from his crouch in front of the fire and dusted his hands on his pant legs. "I won't concern myself with the fire in the future then, Miss Taylor."

He didn't have to be begged to avoid any more reminders of his pain.

"Sergeant Bryant," a sharp voice reprimanded. "How have you come to earn such a rank when you can't follow orders?"

He lifted his gaze to the stairs. Mrs. Taylor raised her eyebrow, emphasizing the question set before him.

"With due respect, ma'am, I don't see any insignia on your sleeve that tells me I have to."

"No," she agreed. "But I *am* a mother." Her voice was strict, but her eyes contained a familiar gentility, much like his own mother's. Yet another reason he couldn't wait to be free of this assignment.

"I'm going to tend the horses," he said, hoping she would give up her crusade. That proved futile.

"You certainly are not. I'll send Benjamin and Gideon to do that," she said. "You're going to bed. I'll bring something to ease your cough and help you sleep."

Ephraim released a sigh. She wasn't going to be easily dissuaded. Problem was, he knew what type of *something* she would bring for his cough. The previous day had afforded him the chance to find that out. A branch of this, a few leaves of that, some roots and bark thrown in. It was a taste he would rather never experience again. If he had to choose between the horrible herbal concoction or facing the entire fury of the Yankee army, he would take the latter. But he had to admit it seemed to work. Three days and his fever was gone, his throat was less swollen and sore, and the pain in his head was subsiding. Now if only he could get back into the saddle. He was going insane here, knowing the others were out doing what he wanted to be doing. But an order was an order. And Patrick Flanagan wasn't a man to have his disregarded.

"I'll drink your tea on the condition that I don't have to stay in bed. I promise you I'm feeling much better."

Mrs. Taylor shook her head in disapproval, but finally relinquished. "All right."

Relief washed over him. It wasn't ideal, but it was better than being confined to bed and captive to his memories.

It was some time before the scuffling sounds of Gideon and Benjamin could be heard descending from upstairs, and even longer until they returned from doing the chores.

Gideon spoke through heavy breaths, just barely running into the house ahead of Benjamin. "I brought your pack in, Sergeant."

Ephraim nodded. "Just set it on the table."

Gideon complied, dropping the pack in the designated place. But as he did, the flap came open and its contents scattered over the floor.

"Sorry," Gideon said, sheepishly bending to retrieve the belongings.

Ephraim cringed and pinched the bridge of his nose. Wherever Gideon went, disaster typically followed. Ephraim tried to have patience, he really did.

But with the circumstances God placed him in it wasn't easy.

"Is this your's?" Gideon stood holding the small book Ephraim recognized to be his Bible. "I've never owned a Bible of my own. Seen the ones that the folks take with 'em to church. But never held one."

"It was my family's," Ephraim said, looking away.

"Who's Remy?"

Adrenaline surged through Ephraim's body. He stood bolt upright. How could one word have such an effect on him?

Gideon had flipped open the cover, revealing writing that ebbed over the page. Ephraim knew every word inscribed on the page from memory. It contained the names of each Bryant man to which the Bible had been passed down. Ephraim had intended on passing it down to Sam one day, but his chance had been snatched away.

Before he could respond or react, Mrs. Taylor tilted her head toward him. "Is it a nickname, Sergeant?"

His face flushed with heat. "Yes, ma'am."

"Unique for your name, isn't it," she asked inquisitively.

"It's after my middle name — Remington. My father was also Ephraim Remington, so it's what my family called me." Ephraim started toward Gideon, jaw tight. He would just as soon have this conversation end before it went anywhere else.

Mariah, who had been setting places at the table, turned her attention to the writing in the book. She squinted. "The Virginia Military Institute?" Her eyes widened as she looked up to him. "You were a cadet there?"

A low whistle came from Benjamin, who leaned forward in anticipation of Ephraim's response.

"For a time. The Bible was a gift upon my entrance to the Institute. Now, if you don't mind," he said, taking the book and closing it with enough force to convey his lack of desire for more questions.

He had already shared more than he wanted. Mrs. Taylor seemed to understand. She cleared her throat and returned to the breakfast preparations.

"Did you sleep well, Gideon?"

"Best night's sleep I've had in a good while, ma'am. It's been ages since we've had a bed to sleep on."

Ephraim turned with a commanding look toward Gideon. "Don't get used to it."

Gideon's face faded into a more somber tone. "No, sir. I won't."

"I'm sure there's no harm in enjoying what you have when you have it," Mariah said pointedly.

Ephraim met her gaze. "Until you don't have it anymore. Then you wish you hadn't ever let yourself grow too fond of it."

"I feel sorry for anyone who lives their lives like that."

"Don't," he said. He looked away, and walked to the window. Frost crept up the corners of the pane, a reminder that winter would soon be upon them. He was dreading every minute of it, especially if he was stuck here for an indefinite time.

Chapter Five

"There, breakfast is hot and ready," Mama said, bringing a steaming plate of cornbread to the table. "Come eat."

The younger boys wasted no time in finding their places around the table, eager to satisfy the hunger in their stomachs.

"Are you coming, Sergeant Bryant?" Mariah asked.

Ephraim barely looked her way. "Thank you. But I have provisions in my pack."

Mama planted a hand on her hip and shook her head. "I've seen what you boys live on, and it isn't fitting to keep a dog alive. Come eat."

"We don't mean to make things harder than they already are for your family. We're here to scout, just like any other mission," Ephraim said. "Hard tack is sufficient for me."

"There isn't a home in our Confederacy that isn't feeling the war's effect. But heaven knows we aren't so destitute we can't take care of our boys." Mama spread a thin layer of golden butter over a piece of cornbread, and placed it at an empty place setting. She turned to the fire, where a steaming kettle puffed the aroma of chicory into the air. In one hand she held a tin cup and with the other poured the hot liquid.

"Didn't you hear me, Sergeant?"

Ephraim hesitated. "Yes, ma'am."

Mama set the tin down. "*Come* and *sit*."

Mariah rose from her seat to tend the simmering pot hanging over the fire. It was an herbal remedy used for centuries in the backwoods of Virginia. Mama had learned a dozen old remedies in the years she had travelled with Papa while he rode the circuit. "You may as well listen," she told Ephraim. "Mama won't allow anything else."

Ephraim reluctantly gave another glance out the window, then took the seat at the table. His eyes closed and his head dropped for a moment.

Mariah looked away. Papa always prayed over their meals. She couldn't help but wonder if he would again. Somewhere deep inside her the fear of the unknown lurked. Nothing was the way it should be. How was she supposed to just accept it all?

How can I trust, Lord? Don't you see what's happening?

Pushing the uneasy thoughts away, Mariah moved to the woodbox inside the door. She reached for the piece on top, but stopped short. From the corner of her eye she noticed Ephraim had risen from his chair and approached beside her.

"Allow me," he said.

"If you must," she replied, stepping to the side.

So he does have some manners.

She bit the inside of her cheek. That may be so, but it still bothered her that there was to be no attempt to free her father. If anyone in the entire country could do so, it would be Flanagan's scouts. Or at least she would have thought so at one time. So why were they sitting here, idly waiting for the federals to make their move? By then it could be too late.

Ephraim stacked a few pieces of wood in the crook of his arm, trying unsuccessfully to hide the wince that came with the pressure on his wound.

"Shouldn't have left it to its own devices," she said.

Ephraim grit his teeth. "Things aren't bad enough, Miss Taylor?"

Mariah planted her hands firmly on her hips. "Well, you shouldn't have. You could've lost it to the gangrene." She shook her head. "It's a wonder you aren't all bedridden with illness or injury. What good will you be doing the cause then?"

"She's right," Mrs. Taylor's voice drifted from the side room where she had disappeared briefly. "You won't be helping the cause any by keeping yourself ill."

Ephraim coughed into his elbow.

"See," Mariah argued, pointing her spoon at him. She moved to the fire once more, stirring the brewing pot.

"Anyone would cough up a lung over whatever it is you're concocting," he defended. "One whiff of that and the whole Yankee army would turn tail and run until they were back in Washington. Someone ought to tell General Lee. The war could be over by Christmas."

She took in a breath and started to speak, but Gideon cut her off. "Someone is coming up the road, sergeant."

Ephraim nearly sprinted to the window and peered out from behind the curtain.

"Are you expecting someone," he asked.

Mariah's heart jumped. Were Amsden and his men returning? She brushed past Gideon and Benjamin, joining him at the window. He stepped aside to allow her a better view. She squinted at the object of concern.

It was a wagon, slowly creaking and groaning its way up the road. An old woman sat atop it, bent over with age. Wrinkles caressed her face, a testament to the many years she had seen. Flyaway wisps of hair peaked out from the simple homespun bonnet she wore.

"It's Ma Fletcher," she said, relieved.

Ephraim still stared hard out the window. "Is it safe?"

Mama dusted her hands off and removed her apron. "No need for concern, Sergeant. She would rather die than aid the Yankees in any way."

Mariah grinned. Nothing could be more true. Ma Fletcher was a force to be reckoned with. She lived a distance away, in Fredericksburg, and was one of the key members of Papa's smuggling ring, which was no doubt the cause for her visit.

The wagon was entering the barnyard now, and Mariah made her way out to greet it. A smile lit the face of the old woman when she saw Mariah.

"I made it through," she said with a chuckle. "Them Bluejackets never stood a chance against me."

"I imagine not," Mariah said.

Ma Fletcher turned and started to climb down, still chattering about the Yankee pickets she eluded. Ephraim stepped up behind her to offer his assistance. But as he reached up to steady her, she gave a startled cry and lost her footing.

Mariah watched in horror as Ma Fletcher fell backward. Ephraim stepped forward just in time to catch her. His injured arm must've borne the brunt of it, because he gave a muffled groan and his face twisted in pain.

"Good heavens, son! You nearly scared me plum out of my skin." Ma Fletcher gasped and clutched her hand to her bosom as he set her on her feet. "Are you trying to send an old woman to her grave?" She smacked him with the stick she carried, obviously recovering her feisty spirit.

Ephraim stepped back. "I'm sorry, ma'am. I didn't mean to startle you. I was trying to help you down."

"Well you did do that, now didn't ye?"

"Yes, ma'am."

Her eyes flitted from him to Mariah and back again. Mariah braced herself for the inevitable question that would be asked. Maybe she should get ahead of it first.

"This is Sergeant Bryant," she explained. "He's ..."

"A friend of Pastor Taylor," Ephraim offered quickly.

Ma Fletcher nodded. "Another supporter of the cause. 'Tis a pleasure to meet you. Though I would suggest you work on making your introductions less of a shock."

With a wince, she pressed a hand to her back and straightened as much as her bones would allow her. "I was hoping your ma would have some herbs for my rheumatism. I'll certainly need it now."

Mariah smiled. "*That* I can promise you. It's one of the few things the Yankees didn't bother. Come in and rest a while."

Ma Fletcher took hold of Ephraim's elbow and shuffled slowly toward the house. Mariah followed.

Once inside, the group gathered at the table, eager to hear of how things fared behind the Yankee blockade. Everyone, that is, except Ephraim, who took residence by the window once more. Mariah could tell he wasn't fully trusting of the situation.

Ma Fletcher took a long sip of the herbal tea Mama had poured for her. Her hands shook slightly as she rested the cup on the table and released a sigh. Her face grew solemn.

"Gabe Thornton told me about Ezekiel," she said, resting a wrinkled hand on Mama's. "I'm sorry, dear."

Mariah looked to the solemn faces gathered around the table, then to Papa's empty chair. Would it ever be filled again? The question hovered above the group, unspoken and unanswered.

"May God help us all," Ma Fletcher continued quietly.

Hmph. God's help seemed far away. Mariah couldn't understand it. None of it made sense. How was she supposed to find rest when everything around her was crumbling?

Mama gave a gracious smile — one that hid her pain. "Ezekiel would not regret his choice to be involved in the work, and neither do I."

"Good," Ma Fletcher stated. "We must carry on where he cannot. It's the reason I've come. The Bibles must get through." She lifted the rim of the cup to her lips and drank.

Mariah fidgeted in her seat. Guilt pricked her heart. If an old woman like Ma Fletcher could find the courage to do something for the Confederacy, couldn't she? But it was too risky. It would only make Papa's situation worse if the Yankees caught her carrying on his work.

She glanced up in time to catch Ephraim looking her way, as if he knew what she was thinking. Irritation replaced the guilt inside her. What did he know of loss and risk?

"Mariah?" Mama's voice broke through her thoughts. "Did you hear me?"

She stared blankly, trying to remember the piece of conversation she had clearly missed.

Benjamin, who must have seen the look exchanged with Ephraim, snickered. "Come on," he said. "The Bibles won't load themselves."

Within half an hour the Bibles were securely loaded in the wagon, ready to make the trek through the lines. Ephraim couldn't help but question the wisdom of sending them with the Fletcher woman. Her intentions were good, he was sure. But she was frail and hindered by age. What would happen to her if the Yankees found the hidden contraband? He wouldn't put it past them to arrest her. And then what?

He would take them himself if Flanagan would let him. But he knew that was out of the question. Smuggling Bibles, while of great value to the cause, was not included in the duties of the Scouts.

Ma Fletcher hobbled from the house, leaning heavily on the crooked walking stick she carried. She stopped where Ephraim was waiting to help her into the wagon again. Pulling on his arm, she leaned close to his ear. "Miss Taylor is a pretty thing, isn't she?"

He could feel his mouth go dry. Her whisper was more of a holler. She may as well shout it from the rooftops. He stammered for something to say in response.

She patted his arm and winked. "A young man like you ought to be courtin' her."

What was he supposed to say to that? Ma Fletcher told no lie when she said Mariah was beautiful. But he had no interest in opening the door for more pain and heartbreak. The family he had loved was taken from him cruelly, and he had no intention of allowing it to happen again. The first step in that process was to keep himself from ever growing too fond of anyone again.

Form no relationships, risk no loss.

Ma Fletcher had moved on now to the arduous task of climbing into the wagon. She paused, one foot resting on the wagon, and raised an eyebrow at him. "You ain't fixin to drop me again, are you?"

Ephraim groaned inwardly at the remembrance of their previous encounter. "No, ma'am."

She eyed him suspiciously again. "Good. See that you don't." Once safely settled onto the weathered old board that created the wagon seat, she winked to them. "Now to see them safely through the lines. I dare say Lincoln would howl like a coyote if he knew this old woman was responsible for thwarting his blockade." She flicked the reins over the backs of the team and started down the road, still chuckling to herself.

Ephraim shook his head. He didn't like her setting off alone. But he couldn't carry every burden. The ones that were his duty to carry were enough to keep him busy. Most pressing for the moment was the fact that he had been at the Taylor farm for three days already and was no wiser to the Yankees' plans. The sooner he made heads or tails of what they were up to meant he could return to his normal duties with the scouts. He couldn't get there soon enough.

He looked back to the group left watching Ma Fletcher disappear down the road. He knew the minute he told Gideon he was leaving he would be pestered with a thousand pleas to accompany him. And if he set out without telling anyone, they would likely call out the entire company of Flanagan Scouts. As much as he wasn't looking forward to the first option, he knew he couldn't send the scouts into a frenzy looking for him. He would just have to put up with Gideon's relentless pleas.

"I'm going for a ride," he said finally. "Miss Taylor, if you'd be so kind as to place the candles in the window like I showed you."

Immediately Gideon perked up. "Sir, will you let me go with you?"

A resounding "no" was waiting on the tip of his tongue, but as the word formed he caught Mariah's gaze.

She crossed her arms. "What's the matter, Sergeant? Don't you ever do anything that requires courage or risk?"

Ephraim froze. The "no" forming on his lips dissolved instantly. Was it a challenge she was giving him?

He set his jaw and put on his hat. "Saddle up."

His gruff tone didn't dampen the excitement that was now evident on Gideon's face. He tore off, disappearing into the barn. Mariah smiled curtly at Ephraim.

"Believe it or not, Miss Taylor, I'm not the ogre you think I am."

"Perhaps then, Sergeant Bryant," she said pointedly, "you ought to tell your face that more often."

"Very funny."

She turned to the house, skirts swishing around her ankles. "I wasn't trying to be."

"Ready, Sergeant," Gideon called.

He grimaced. This was going to be a long day.

At first the excursion was kept in total silence. Which was just fine as far as Ephraim was concerned. Senseless chatter wasn't something he was fond of.

A fading mural of fiery hues canvased the sky above them, and the crunch of leaves filled their ears. Ephraim would enjoy every last minute of autumn before facing the misery of winter.

"Do you like her?" Gideon had turned to Ephraim, gaze unrelenting.

"Who?"

"Miss Taylor," Gideon said.

The remark sent a cloud of somberness over Ephraim. Like Miss Taylor in a *romantic* way? In *any* way? Of course not. He had no desire to be thinking of starting a family. Certainly not with a woman who would just as soon shoot him as have to look at him.

"No."

Gideon continued on, seemingly unfazed by Ephraim's short reply. "They're good people, aren't they? I always wondered what it would be like to have a family like them."

Hmph. Nothing to set your heart on, kid. The sooner you learn that is for the better.

"Do you think I might ever have one?"

Ephraim gave an annoyed sigh. "Have *what*?"

"A family," Gideon said. He looked at Ephraim with such sincere eyes that Ephraim couldn't bring himself to respond in his usual manner. When Gideon joined the scouts he had informed them of his status as an orphan, but hadn't discussed it much.

"I don't even have a surname." Gideon's brow furrowed as he spoke. "What's it like, Sergeant? To have a name that belongs to your family, I mean."

Ephraim's face softened some. How could he tell Gideon that what he wanted so desperately was only a painful reminder that Ephraim wished he didn't have to carry? Every time Flanagan or one of the scouts called him by his last name, it brought up the memory of a family he hadn't been given enough time with. It was nothing to envy.

"It's not so special," he said, voice husky.

"It is if you've never had one," Gideon replied quietly.

After scouting the woodland and Yankee encampment on the outskirts of town, they arrived at the base of a heavily wooded knoll. From the top, they would have a clear view of town. Ephraim held up his hand to signal a halt. He dismounted and crouched down, slowly cresting the hill while keeping a low profile. Gideon followed, to Ephraim's chagrin.

The field glasses he had brought from his saddle bag offered him a view of what was happening. He hadn't seen an area more plagued with Yanks. They were all over the once-quiet little southern town. And from intelligence the other scouts had gathered, the encampment on the outskirts was brimming over.

What are they planning?

He moved his gaze toward the county jail that had been taken over by the Yankees. Within its walls Pastor Taylor awaited his trial. If the presiding judge and jury was anyone other than Jacob Amsden, Ephraim would say there was a fair chance he would be released. But Amsden was a different type of man — one who had no qualms about arresting a preacher. Or hanging one for that matter. It would take a miracle for the charges to be dropped.

"Can I look?"

Ephraim lowered the glasses, acutely aware that his young charge was hovering much too close. Gideon shrank back with a sheepish smile. "Sorry."

Ephraim handed him the field glasses, gaze still fixed on the occupied town. What did it all mean?

"Hey! That's Miss Taylor," Gideon exclaimed.

Ephraim straightened. "What? Let me see."

Sure enough. Standing on the boardwalk across from the jail, Mariah stood as if trying to decide her next move. His heart lurched. He didn't like the feeling he was getting. Their plan was for the Taylors to spend as little time as possible in town to avoid drawing unwanted attention. He could see she listened to that strategy well.

Chapter Six

Mariah drew a deep breath of the cool air. Her legs felt as though they would give out underneath her. Did she truly have the courage to walk into the jail now run by the Yankees?

It was hard not to despise them. When they had come it had erased any sense of normalcy that lingered in spite of the war. Sorrow hung above the little town like clouds threatening rain. Martial law ruled now and their freedoms were threatened.

She watched as a soldier left the building and another went in. If it weren't for the necessity that drove this embarkment, she wouldn't care to ever come within a mile of a Yankee, much less have to ask them for permission to visit her father. But as it stood, she had little choice.

With a breath and a prayer she started toward the building, trying her best to walk with confidence. As she reached for the doorknob, the wooden door swung inward. A stout figure clad in Federal blue blocked her from entering. Amsden appeared as surprised to see her as she was him. "Miss Taylor," he said curtly.

Mariah poised herself. "Captain."

"Let's not beat around the bush. I assume you're here because of your father."

"I'd like to see him if I might."

Amsden planted a fist on his hip. "I'm afraid I can't allow that. He's being held on very serious charges against the Union, as I'm sure you know. No visitors until after trial."

A rush of anger turned Mariah's cheeks crimson. "He's my father, and I demand to see him. What cause do you have for preventing me?"

Amsden brushed past her, closing the door tightly behind him. He turned to face her, expression smug. "I don't need to explain myself to some impertinent Reb female. Now I suggest you go home before you get yourself into trouble." He spun sharply and strode off the boardwalk onto the dusty street. He called flippantly over his shoulder, "Don't bother trying to convince the guard inside to let you in. I've already left orders with him."

Hmph. Since when has that ever stopped one of us impertinent Rebs?

She had come this far and she wasn't going to back out now. She lifted the basket higher on her arm and opened the door with determination. Directly in front of her sat a desk, and behind it a surly looking soldier peering down his long nose at her.

"Well?" He growled.

"I'm here to see my father, sir."

"You the preacher's daughter?"

"Yes, sir."

He looked back down at the stick he was whittling. "Well then you can just forget about it. Be on your way."

Mariah set her basket down on the desk, hard enough to draw his attention again. "What harm could there be in allowing me just five minutes?"

He heaved a sigh as though it was an unbearable burden. "I have orders, miss. And I'm not about to let the likes of you get me into trouble."

She thought for a moment. What was it that could make a man so sour?

"Sir, do you have any children?"

He continued whittling, seemingly unfazed by the conversation. "Nope. And I'm not looking to hear no sad story about it neither." By now he had risen and made his way around the corner of the desk. He took her elbow and moved toward the door. "For the last time, be on your way, miss."

Mariah pulled her arm away from his grip. "I'm able to find my own way to the door, and I would kindly ask you to keep your hands to yourself."

He held up his hands in defense. "Meant no harm to you. Just be on your way."

A sinking feeling filled her stomach. Her first covert mission for her nation and she was failing at it miserably. She stopped short of the door and turned to face him once again.

"If you won't permit me to see him, may I at least ask to be given his Bible?" Her eyes moved to the old Book perched precariously on the edge of the desk. "It would be of some comfort to my mother."

The soldier hesitated briefly, unsure of how to answer. She bit the inside of her cheek.

Finally he released a heavy sigh and picked up the book. "All right, you can take it. But for the love of all that's good, miss, please be on your way before the captain comes back."

Mariah wasted no time in securing the book beneath the cloth covering her basket. The farther she got from this place and these men would be for the best.

Once safely a distance from the building, she turned to study it again. Somewhere within its walls Papa awaited his fate. If they ever discovered he was involved with the Flanagan Scouts, it would surely mean a death sentence.

She left town quickly, having no desire to be reminded of the occupation they were under. The road was mostly vacant, which afforded her ample room to skirt around the mud puddles and ruts that marred it.

She turned her face toward the warm rays filtering through the canopy of trees. It felt good — calm and assuring in spite of all that had transpired. Heaven knew she needed some calm and assurance in her life. She tried to rest in who God was, just like Papa had taught her from the time she was a babe. But she hadn't ever found it so hard as it was now. Now, when everything that was once secure and certain was anything but. Change had come so quickly with the start of the war that she'd had no time to sort through it all. She had asked God to teach her to be at rest, but so far the only answer she'd received was more unrest. At least for now she could relish the peace of enjoying the last bit of autumn sunshine before winter set in.

The thunder of hoofbeats reverberated in the air as two riders on horseback galloped up, coming to an abrupt halt beside her. A spray of cold mud splattered over her.

"What did you think you were doing," Ephraim demanded, sliding from his mount.

Mariah sucked in a breath and prayed for patience. "What was *I* thinking? What were *you* thinking?" She wiped at the muddy mixture sliding down her forehead.

Ephraim ignored her question, intent on gaining an answer to his own. "The more attention you draw to your family the less likely your father is to be acquitted. Do you really want the likes of Jacob Amsden looking at your family that close? I've had a run-in with him before, and believe me, you don't."

Mariah finished clearing the mud spatters, then cleaned her hands on her skirt. Was it concern she detected in Ephraim's voice? More likely it was his usual grouchiness shining through again.

"Jacob Amsden is already well aware of my family, and there's nothing so unusual about a woman requesting to see her father."

Gideon leaned on his saddle horn, intent on the exchange taking place. "Did you see him?"

"No. But they gave me his Bible."

Ephraim's gaze penetrated through her, but he said nothing. It was obvious he was not pleased or impressed. He shook his head, choosing for once to keep his thoughts to himself, and motioned for her to mount Shenandoah.

"Climb up," he said.

"I'm not about to get on a horse with *you*."

He planted a fist on his hip. "The feeling is mutual, miss. My intention was for you to ride her alone. Unless you prefer to walk?"

"I never said I didn't want to walk. I walked into town, and I'm sure I can walk back."

Ephraim thrust the reins toward her. "Don't complain I have no manners if you aren't willing to accept them when they're present."

"But what are you going to do," she asked in protest.

"Walk," he said, dryly. "Unless I happen across a friendly Yankee willing to give me a lift to camp."

She scrunched up her face at his sarcasm. "Very funny."

"I wasn't trying to be," he repeated her words from earlier.

At this she took the reins offered her and pulled herself into the saddle. Ephraim gave a gruff nod, albeit still without so much as a hint of pleasantness. "I'll be along later. Have something I need to talk to Flanagan about."

"Can't we do anything?"

Ephraim took the tin that steamed with the aroma of chicory. He watched the steam rise from the cup, curl and twist, then dissipate entirely. Flanagan was studying him intently.

"What do you want us to do?"

Ephraim set the tin down and stood, pacing restlessly. "I don't know."

"You want us to do something, but you don't know what?"

When Flanagan put it that way even Ephraim had a hard time believing what he was asking for. How could Flanagan *act* if he didn't even know what he was acting on? Truth was, Ephraim himself didn't know what he expected Flanagan to do. He paused, kicking a rock in his path with the frustration he felt inside him.

"Why can't we break him out?"

Chris, who had been sitting quiet through much of the time, raised both eyebrows and his eyes widened. His look said what no one would out loud.

Flanagan coughed into his fist, searching the ground before him as if the answer lay somewhere in it. "I admire your tenacity. But that's plain stupid, son."

The statement from Flanagan wasn't anything Ephraim didn't already know. But that didn't mean he relished his commander informing him of it.

"Why?"

Flanagan looked at him in bewilderment. "Are you daft, boy? Have you seen the troop of Bluedevils camped in town?" He stepped into the path Ephraim was pacing, bringing him to a halt. "And you want to break Taylor out for *what*? To let the Yanks know he's got bigger charges against him than just smuggling? *Think about it*, son. How do you think they're gonna treat Taylor and his family if Flanagan's Scouts go tearing in there to save him?"

"But, sir, think what they will they do to him if they find him guilty of smuggling contraband," Chris said, coming to Ephraim's defense.

Frustration welled inside Ephraim. Of course he knew that what the captain said was sound logic. Of course he knew that they were a band of marked men, and that it carried guilt by association for any who dared aid them. He knew all those things, and yet it wasn't right for a man of Pastor Taylor's integrity to suffer unjustly with no hope of rescue.

Flanagan tilted his head. "What's gotten into you?"

He slid his hat from his head, and gripped it tightly in his hands. "The Taylors miss him real bad, sir. Miss Taylor went to the jail today to see him, but they wouldn't let her. I figured there ought to be something we could do."

At this Chris and Flanagan exchanged a glance.

"Miss Taylor?" they asked in unison.

Chris was incredulous. "The same Miss Taylor whom you said can't stand you?"

Ephraim crossed his arms. "All right, all right. Forget I ever asked."

They were right. He was growing too invested, and if he wasn't careful, it would haunt him later. It wasn't like he owed the Taylors anything. He hadn't even really wanted to come talk to Flanagan about it. But it was his duty to protect innocence — something his conscience wasn't willing to let him forget. It was an innate tug that wouldn't leave, constantly reminding him to look out for those who couldn't look out for themselves. There was something in Miss Taylor's eyes on the road outside of town that fueled it.

Flanagan clapped him on the back. "I know you want to help them. And we will. If it comes down to the Yanks hanging him, you know I won't abide by it. But we're going to wait and hear the verdict of the trial first. For all we know they may only fine him and let him go. As difficult as it may be to leave him there for a time, it's in his best interest."

"Yessir." Ephraim saluted, turning sharply and leaving. Chris caught up with him in short order. "So how *are* things going," he asked.

"With what?"

Chris gave an exaggerated sigh. "With the Taylors, of course."

"I'll be glad when I'm back at camp permanently," Ephraim grumbled.

"Any particular reason," Chris asked. "Or is it just because you don't want to admit that maybe you're growing fond of them?"

"Chris, you know where I stand on that. I am not looking to gain a family."

"I know, I know. You intend on ending up a grouchy old miser, attached to no one and nothing. Well if you don't watch out, you may get your wish."

Ephraim crossed his arms. "It's more likely I won't survive the war, in which case it won't matter."

Many men his age had already fallen in the battles. What was to prevent him from being among them? It was a grim thought, but it didn't make it any less a strong possibility. The odds of surviving were slim.

Chris shrugged. "Suit yourself. But when you end up alone and miserable for the rest of your life, don't say I didn't warn you."

Chris had never been one to mince words, regardless of whether his opinion was solicited or not. Ephraim bit the inside of his cheek to keep from sharing the retort that came to his mind. Chris knew nothing about what it was like to be in Ephraim's boots. Grief had a way of searing itself into one's heart so that they never forgot the pain that caused it. How could anyone, including himself, expect it to be forgotten?

Chapter Seven

November's warm hues quickly faded into the dull and cold tones of winter. It was shaping up to be an unusually cold one for their little part of the world. Every morning frost sparkled on the windows and covered the world outside, and in the evenings the wind howled with the threat of harsh months ahead of them. Mariah rather enjoyed it when the seasons turned. It seemed to always bring the family closer together. They would spend the long dark nights curled up near the fire, telling all manner of stories and tales, and listening to Papa read from his Bible. Then each would scurry to their beds before the warmth of the fire had melted away and burrow deep under a mountain of quilts.

This winter was bound to be different though. The family wouldn't be all together, thanks to the war. If she had the choice, she would spend it tucked away in bed, ignoring the war and all the problems it brought, and waiting for the spring thaw. But even if she had that option, Benjamin wouldn't allow it to happen.

"Get up," he persisted, shaking her by the shoulders.

Mariah groaned and rolled over, pulling the blankets over her head. "Go away."

Her efforts were to no avail. Benjamin tugged back the blankets and shook her again. "You know what today is?"

She sighed. Once Benjamin got a bee in his bonnet about something, there was no dissuading him. She would just have to resign herself to getting up and facing the day. She threw back her quilt and sat up, her face likely saying everything she wanted to and more. "It's Monday, unfortunately."

"It's the first day of December. Which means it's almost Christmas—"

"Hmph. Twenty-five days hardly constitutes 'almost'."

Benjamin crossed his arms disapprovingly. "Which *means* ..." he emphasized, "we need to decorate."

"All right, all right. Let me get dressed." She shooed him out of the room.

It was a long standing tradition that every December first Papa would take them to hunt for the perfect Christmas decorations and tree. They would gather boughs of greenery, berries, and pinecones. Their voices would carry through the woods with the wings of carols and hymns. But this year nothing was the same it had been. Papa wasn't here to take them, and she didn't much feel like singing. For Benjamin, though, she would go and carry on as if it was any year gone by. He deserved that much at least.

That was the mindset that she carried with her downstairs and into the toasty warm kitchen. Everyone else was already awake and starting breakfast. She slid into her place at the table, taking the bowl of grits offered her.

"Aren't you eating," Benjamin asked Ephraim.

He was kneeling at the fireplace, adding more wood to the blaze. At Benjamin's question he lifted his head, eyes meeting Mariah's and quickly looking away. "I don't eat breakfast. But I'm obliged for the offer," he said with a hint of a smile. Mariah was shocked it didn't crack his face to do so.

Benjamin leaned his elbow on the table, studying Ephraim. He was curious of all things regarding the scouts. "How long have you been up?"

Gideon piped up this time. "Sergeant Bryant never sleeps past the sun."

Of course he doesn't. He seems the type to actually enjoy mornings.

"Most days he's been up for a few hours before the sun is," Gideon continued. "Ain't that right?"

Ephraim stood and brushed off the soot from his hands. "It just seems that way because you barely make morning roll call."

"I can't blame you, Gideon," Mariah said, pointedly looking at Ephraim. "Mornings are awful."

"Mornings are *useful*, Miss Taylor. Especially when you're in the work we do."

Mariah sucked in a breath, holding back her thoughts. He had to be the most ill tempered man she had acquainted. Did he ever smile?

Benjamin cleared his throat. "We're going to gather decorations for Christmas this morning, sergeant. Will you go with us?"

Mariah furrowed her brow. Was she imagining it or had Ephraim's face gone ashen? His eyes were suddenly lifeless, and for a moment she thought she could see his heart break in the emotion written on his face. But he quickly regained composure and the rigid professionalism he always bore.

"I'm not much for Christmas, but I'll accompany you."

Breakfast was finished, the dishes washed and dried, and they set out on their mission. Benjamin and Gideon jabbered on about any and every topic as they made their way into the woods near the farm. Mariah noticed Ephraim stayed silent and attentively alert to any danger. The Yankees didn't often grace this part of the forest, as they knew it was the scout's territory. Of late they had mainly been staying close to town. But there was always the possibility that there could be trouble.

"You know you didn't have to come," Mariah stated.

"You're my charges until Flanagan says otherwise. It's my job to see you're protected." His eyes never left their surroundings as he spoke.

Charges. Hmph.

"Do you anticipate trouble?"

"The scouts who stay alive always do. I don't reckon the Federals care much if I'm hunting Christmas trees or spying out secrets. I already had one run-in with them this year, and I'd just as soon not make it a habit."

Mariah switched the basket she carried to the other hand. "You're a scout, not a spy."

He merely glanced to the side for a brief moment. "Doesn't seem there's much difference in the Yanks' eyes."

"The difference is whether or not you die if you are captured," Mariah said.

"They'd just as soon hang me regardless of the presence of a uniform."

Her heart skipped a beat. Why, she couldn't say. He was no one special. Only a man serving his nation like thousands of other Confederate boys — and an irritating one at that. But still the thought of him dying made her blood run cold.

"Don't speak such things."

He turned his gaze away from the woods and studied her for a moment. "I knew the risks when I took the job. Everyone knows hanging is the death of a spy. I figure it can't be any worse than lying on a forsaken battlefield, slowly bleeding out. I signed up for this, Miss Taylor."

Icy fingers of fear and unease wrapped around her, rivaling the frigid wind. She pulled her shawl closer around her body. They both knew hanging was no way to die. Slow and agonizing, it was a death she would wish on no one.

"I — hope that never happens," she whispered, barely loud enough to be heard above the rustling branches and wind.

But he heard. She knew he heard. He seemed to flinch a little, as if her well wishes stung. His eyes met hers for a second of time, then reverted back to the forestry.

They had reached a grove of winterberry. Its vibrant red berries were a stark contrast against the bleak and barren ground. Mariah could already see them adorning the mantel above the fireplace and the windowsills. Later, they would string some of them into a garland with chestnuts to decorate the tree. They began filling their baskets.

"We wish you a merry Christmas, we wish you a merry Christmas!"

Mariah joined Benjamin and Gideon in the familiar old carol. Once it was finished they sang another and another. For a time Mariah almost could've forgotten their troubles and the war.

"We just need some music to accompany us," Mariah said with a grin.

Gideon perked up at the comment. "Sergeant Bryant plays. Captain Flanagan often asks him to play for us at camp."

Mariah looked hopefully to Ephraim. "Would you play for us, Sergeant? It's been so long since we've had music in the house."

He seemed embarrassed to have such attention. He looked away and shook his head. "No. I don't play carols." He stalked off in the opposite direction without another word.

Mariah blinked. She hadn't expected him to give her such a direct answer, and certainly not that answer. Benjamin looked warily toward her, his bewilderment apparent. Gideon, however, only watched Ephraim with a look of disappointment mixed with sadness. Anyone could see how much he idolized Ephraim and longed to gain his favor. Except, of course, Ephraim himself.

Mariah retrieved her basket from its perch on the ground beside her and followed in the direction Ephraim had taken. He was as unpredictable as the Rappahannock, constantly making her wonder what was around the next bend. There were times over the course of time he had spent in their home that he seemed almost happy and jovial. But those were sparse compared to these moments when he seemed ancient beyond his years — as if his soul had grown far too old and serious while his body was still young.

The abrupt end to their berry picking didn't impact Gideon and Benjamin for long. They walked along ahead, laughing and jabbering as boys will do. But an awkward silence hung between Ephraim and herself.

"Why?" She almost surprised herself with the boldness in her question. She studied his face. Expressionless. And life had gone from his eyes.

"Because I don't."

"But Christmas is such a peaceful time — or it should be." Mariah ignored the fact that she herself was struggling to find peace this Christmastide.

He stopped abruptly and turned to face her. "I'm glad you've had that experience. But there is nothing peaceful in Christmas for me, Miss Taylor. Nothing."

"Surely there must be *something* that is beautiful to you about it."

"Beautiful?" He grunted. "I *buried* my family at Christmas. Do you think there's anything beautiful about that?"

Mariah stammered to find an answer, regretting having pushed the issue. She understood now why it was said the eyes were the window of the soul, for in that moment his own were an intricate mural of the sorrows, pains, and wounds that painted his. Something inside her ached on his behalf.

"I'm sorry," she said gently. "I'll pray you find peace this Christmas, Sergeant."

Let him find rest for his soul, Lord Jesus.

Chapter Eight

Ten days passed. Ten days of watching nothing but the wind in the trees and the freezing sleet come down. Ephraim stacked two more pieces of firewood in Gideon's arms. He dragged in a deep breath and filled his own arms with firewood, following close behind Gideon. Instantly he was greeted with the savory scent of stewing vegetables. He knelt beside the fireplace, careful not to rest for too long. Though he was mostly recovered, he still didn't have full strength. And something told him that Mrs. Taylor would be able to notice a sniffle from a mile away. She had that doctoring look in her eye.

He cringed with the pressure of lifting one of the logs onto the fire. A shower of sparks shot upward into the inky blackness of the chimney. He watched them extinguish one by one, his mind lulled by the atmosphere around him. Mrs. Taylor was softly humming as she worked. Gideon and Benjamin were engrossed in a game they had made up, their voices carrying through the house. A peacefulness seemed to encapsulate all of it. Though how deep it went, he wasn't certain.

He had forgotten what a home felt like. He *missed* what it felt like. Which was exactly why he wanted to go back to camp. He didn't want such a poignant reminder of all he had lost.

"And what of your family, Sergeant?"

Ephraim looked up briefly, thoughts interrupted by Mrs. Taylor's voice. "I'm sorry, ma'am?"

"'Tis the Christmastide," she said as though he hadn't missed the entire first half of the conversation. "Surely you must miss your family even more this time of year."

A pit formed in his stomach. The peacefulness of a moment prior was shattered once again. Mariah met his gaze, the knowledge of their conversation on the topic lingering between unspoken.

"The Christmastide is only another month to weather the winter, ma'am. And as to a family, I don't have one anymore."

Mrs. Taylor's face softened. She nodded with a tender gentleness so reminiscent of his own mother that it made him ache with homesickness. "I'm very sorry."

He shrugged and placed another log on the crackling fire. "Makes no difference. That's why I'm a scout. It's best not to have family ties holding you back from doing your job. That's what the captain always says."

"Remember that we will be here waiting for you."

He squeezed his eyes shut, pushing the memory far away. He didn't want to remember. He wanted to shake free from the past for good. It was better this way.

They turned their attention to the door as Benjamin ran in. "Yankees coming up the road."

Ephraim scrambled to his feet and pulled his revolver from his belt. "How many?"

"More than I can count."

"Where's Gideon," Mariah asked, worry creeping into her expression.

No sooner had she spoken, then Gideon burst through the door. Already the rumble of boots on the ground was making its way to them.

"We can pray that they are only passing by," Mrs. Taylor said.

Ephraim kept silent, watching the road. He knew better than to trust that the Yankees would ever simply be passing by. Too many farms had been raided since they invaded. Wherever the Yanks passed through you could count on thievery and trouble.

Their dusty blue coats almost looked gray in the fading light of day. From a distance someone might have mistaken them for Confederate boys. But as the old saying went, things aren't always as they seem. Beneath the coating of dust stood true blue uniforms that represented ideals so foreign to his own.

They marched in neat columns, like a mighty river. Ephraim counted in his head the number of men passing. But they only kept coming. This was something worth telling the captain about.

He turned from the window and lifted his sword belt from the table. "I think the captain needs to know about this. I don't like the looks of it. We've been waiting for the Federals to make a move across the river, and this might be it. If we slip out the back and take the long way around, we should be able to get to camp all right."

Gideon headed for the peg near the door and grabbed his hat.

"Wouldn't it be safer if Gideon stayed?" Mariah asked.

Ephraim finished strapping on his sheath and took his own hat that Gideon offered. "I might need him to be a courier, Miss Taylor. Apart from that, he joined the scouts. If we stayed home any time there was a chance of danger, the country would be in a fine fix."

She made no further argument, but he could see the worry in her eyes. He turned away, firmly planting his hat on his head. A final check to ensure his revolver was in its place at his side sent him on his way, Gideon following behind. They picked their way through the wooded land north of the old house, then broke into a gallop once far enough that their hoofbeats would not be heard by the troop marching along the road. With the advantage of being on horseback, they would make it in time to cut them off.

Mariah bit her lip. Sergeant Bryant and Gideon would be testing the limits to get across in front of the Yankees without detection. She breathed a silent prayer for their safety.

"Do you think they'll make it?"

Mama turned from the fireplace where she had kept herself busy kindling the fire. Her lips turned into a smile that illuminated her eyes, though worry lines remained across her forehead. "How many trips like this do you suppose he has taken without being caught? I think they'll make it all right."

Mariah bit her lip. "According to Gideon he's the best scout in all of Virginia."

"Are you inclined to agree with him?" A sparkle twinkled in Mama's eyes.

"No ... I mean ... I don't know," Mariah said, tripping over her words. She directed her gaze into the steadily growing darkness. Silence followed. Then she spoke again. "He's quiet so often. Sometimes I think there is more hurt hiding behind his gruff demeanor than anything else. Have you noticed it too?"

Mama pulled her shawl from its hook near the door and wrapped it around her shoulders. "I suppose everyone hides their hurt behind one thing or another, but he does seem to carry a heavy burden, doesn't he?" Her skirts swept over the floor as she walked, coming behind Mariah and gently braiding her long strands.

Mariah closed her eyes. She never got tired of Mama doing her hair. Steady hands that so skillfully and tenderly weaved the strands into a braid just as she did when Mariah was a child and she would tie them with a string and leave them to move freely as Mariah ran in the woods and fields. Now that she was a grown woman, Mama pinned them securely in a coil at the nape of her neck.

When she had finished she turned Mariah and met her gaze. "He's a good, just man and I believe his intentions are pure. He leads with strength and humility. It's natural to find those qualities attractive."

Mariah blushed. How did mother always know? *Was* it attraction that she felt toward him? If that question had been posed the very first time they met, she likely would've found it insane. He had seemed so harsh in those first meetings, but maybe she was the one who had been harsh.

"And I dare say he finds *you* attractive," Mama said, a knowing sparkle in her eyes.

"He doesn't show it. Hardly even gives me the time of day."

Mama shook her head. "He does show it. When he carries the firewood in for you. When he insists on accompanying you when you leave the house. When he steals an admiring glance toward you when you turn away."

"He does?" Her heart increased its beating. "What do I do?"

"You stand still and wait for the Lord. If it is his will, he'll make it known in his time. For now though there is much more to think of."

Mariah nodded, mind still swirling with the possibility that Sergeant Bryant found her attractive. "I'll place the candles in case they return tonight."

It was hard to say how long they would be gone. Sometimes they disappeared for days without any word. Other times they were back within a short time. She carried the two candles to the windowsill. Their glow illuminated the glass. She watched them flicker and dance until something outside the window caught her eye. Could it be? She looked again. Yes, this time she was certain.

"Mama," she breathed. "It's snowing."

She was out the door and into the night before any response could be given. Fluffy snowflakes swirled on the wind, landing gently on the ground. It wasn't so common for them to get snow. The mountain elevations were usually where the snow fell, but this winter had already proven to be much more harsh.

She looked up to the well of blackness from which it fell. Icy cold flakes landed on her face, melting into water droplets. It was silent, and for the first time since Papa's arrest, it almost seemed peaceful. Her breath was beginning to freeze in puffs in the air.

The silence was broken by the sound of hoofbeats on the road, approaching quickly. She squinted to see in the dark. Could Ephraim and Gideon already be returning? Maybe they hadn't been able to make it to camp and turned back.

She froze in place, her blood running cold as the riders approached.

"Mama," she called, her throat growing tight. She wasn't apt to soon forget the last time a rogue group of Yankees had come. Her hands gripped the edges of her shawl tightly. A shiver swept over her, but not from the cold.

Jacob Amsden dismounted and strode toward her, his men following suit. His face matched the iciness of the wind.

"Miss Taylor," he acknowledged with a snide voice. "Expecting someone else?"

Mariah narrowed her gaze. "What is it you want?"

He placed one of his boots on the step and leaned forward on his knee. "That's not real polite, now is it?"

She stepped backward, out of his reach. His breath smelled sour and repulsive. And his manners were even more so.

"I think we'll come in and sit a spell. Didn't your mama say she never turns people away from her table?" He stepped up to the door and twisted the knob to open it. He motioned for her to enter ahead of him.

Mariah crossed her arms, eyes squinted into a glare.

"What on earth is the meaning of this?" Mama planted her hands firmly on her hips. She raised her eyebrow in a questioning look to Amsden.

He strutted in and took a seat not offered him. "Mrs. Taylor," he said. "How nice to be in your company again. My men and I will be staying for a while. Why don't you make some coffee and dinner?"

Mariah cocked her head. "Why don't *you* learn some manners?"

Mama lifted her hand just enough to signal Mariah to hold her peace. "Captain, you're bold to assume we have the luxury of coffee at our disposal. Had you brought some from your army's brimming coffers, I would gladly make it. But as it stands, you'll have to go without."

Amsden started to answer her, but Mariah wasn't listening. She had one thought on her mind. The candles. They were still brightly glowing in the window. If Ephraim and Gideon returned right now, they would be walking into a trap. She shifted her gaze to the soldiers Amsden had brought with him. They were all preoccupied listening to their commander droll on and on.

She slowly moved toward the window, eyes still intent on the occupying soldiers. When she reached it, she cautiously picked up the candlesticks and moved toward the kitchen. Her hands shook with the fear of being found out, and her mouth had gone dry long ago.

"Miss Taylor."

Her heart dropped with a sickening thud. All eyes were now on her. Amsden's eyes carried a cold knowingness.

"Where are you taking the candles?"

She looked down to the evidence in her hands, then back to him. "I'm moving them where they will be better suited."

He stood and sauntered toward her. "You see, I've noticed something rather odd with those candles. Only on certain nights does your kitchen window hold the glow of two candles."

She squared her shoulders and lifted her chin. "Is that so odd? Most people use candles at night."

Amsden nodded, allowing his eyes to dance over the room. "Why this window, Miss Taylor? If you were in need of extra light, would it not be in that corner, there by the table?"

Mariah allowed her face to remain blank. Was he merely guessing at their secret or did he know?

He smiled wickedly and took the candles from her. The flames flickered and almost went out as he moved them back to the windowsill. "I have a theory that I think we'll test. I think that there is a method to your madness after all. Let's wait and see who shows up, shall we? I warn you, Miss Taylor, if it is one of the Flanagan Scouts you'll be arrested with them."

Lord, keep them away tonight. Please don't let them come back.

He turned back after placing the candles. "Please, sit down."

Mama motioned for her to sit beside her. Mariah locked eyes with her, silently screaming the fears that held her captive. If Ephraim and Gideon came back ...

Mama squeezed her hand knowingly. "Be still."

And know that I am God.

Mariah finished the verse silently. Mama seldom lost her head in situations of danger. She and Papa had worked for so long in the Underground that it came second hand to them. They always told their children that God would never fail them. They need only to be still and, in so doing, rest in the peace of God. But Mariah had never come by that easily. She fidgeted anxiously in the chair.

Amsden leaned back nonchalantly and placed his mud-caked boots on the table. Mariah glowered. He had to be the most disgusting man she had ever acquainted.

"I get the feeling you don't like me, Miss Taylor."

She bit back the reply that wanted to come. She found him loathsome.

"I don't find your willingness to wrongfully arrest a Man of God very likable."

"Your father was caught smuggling contraband into enemy hands. He should be hanged as a traitor."

Mariah pursed her lips in a tight line. "Is it so awful for a man to want Holy Scriptures placed into the hands of young men going to their deaths?"

Captain Amsden crossed his arms. His gaze penetrated right through her. "The young men going to their deaths should have thought of that before starting a war."

"What is it your government is afraid of? If your cause is so just, I would think they would be anxious to ensure that every Confederate soldier was given a copy of the Word."

"There's no way to ensure that weapons aren't being smuggled in with Bible shipments."

Mariah crossed her arms. "Tell me, Captain, when was the last time you saw a rifle small enough to fit inside a Bible?"

The grin on Amsden's face disintegrated into a frown. "I'm not interested in discussing technicalities, miss. I don't make the rules."

"No, but you do make the arrests," Mama said curtly.

It was near impossible for Mariah to keep her mind off the candles flickering and dancing carelessly, as if they may not be the downfall of Flanagan's scouts this night. She bit her lower lip.

Private Carrigen turned away from the window. "Riders coming, sir."

Mariah's heart lurched. Suddenly she felt sick with nausea. She stole a look at mother, who maintained a composed demeanor.

Amsden stood and drew his sidearm. "I advise you not to try to warn them in any way, ladies. My men will fire on them if you do."

Please, let them see that something is wrong. Oh God, they'll hang if they're caught.

Amsden and the others took their places out of sight in the room. It was a waiting game to see who would come through the door. Mariah tried to calm the panic within her. Maybe it wasn't them.

The logic inside her drowned out the hope her thoughts tried to offer. The sound of boots on the porch echoed through the room. Then a knock on the door. Amsden turned the knob and let the door swing open.

Ephraim and Chris stepped in, brushing off their coats and removing their hats. "It's colder than Lincoln's heart tonight," Chris quipped.

Where was Gideon?

But there wasn't time to find an answer to that question. At least not yet. Amsden pushed the door closed behind them, his men taking their places to ensure Ephraim and Chris had nowhere to run.

"That's unfortunate for you boys," Amsden said in reply to Chris. "It'll be a cold walk to jail."

Chapter Nine

Ephraim froze, eyes locked on the fireplace in front of him. That was a voice he would never forget. He remembered it from several months before, when he had found himself in Yankee hands.

From behind them the figure emerged in Federal uniform.

Ephraim's stomach sank and his face flushed with anger. This was not how he anticipated the evening to go. Their eyes met. Recognition hit Amsden's face like a mini-ball.

"Amsden," Ephraim breathed. Who was more shocked by the meeting he couldn't tell. But Amsden soon recovered his surprise and an evil grin spread over his face with the realization of just what the situation was.

"Well, well, well. This is better than I thought it would be. You know I vowed I would kill you if I ever got my hands on your sorry hide again."

Ephraim clenched his teeth as Amsden confiscated the weapons they each bore. Anger built inside him like storm clouds gathering on a summer's eve. "The feeling is mutual."

"Well then, I guess it's a good thing I found you first," he smirked. "And you've even brought one of your men with you."

Ephraim grit his teeth. He wondered silently how long they would keep them in jail before hanging them. Something told him it wouldn't be long. Amsden would likely be the one to do it.

It's gotta be better than slowly bleeding out on a battlefield.

His words to Mariah echoed in his mind. In this moment he would've preferred the battlefield to being hung by a man like Jacob Amsden.

A shout caught the attention of those gathered in the room. Benjamin had made a dash for the open door, but one of Amsden's men grabbed him. Benjamin provided a sharp blow to the soldier's shin. The Yank released a howl and bent to grip his injured leg, releasing his captive in the process. Benjamin disappeared into the night.

The smirk plastered on Amsden's face disappeared. "You idiot," he shouted at the soldier. "Go catch him!"

The soldier complied, limping along gingerly.

Amsden spun to face Ephraim and Chris. "Tie them up while I decide what I want to do with them," he barked to his men.

"Sir, is this necessary?" Mrs. Taylor spoke with confidence that barely seemed to quiver. Ephraim supposed she had had to be brave with an outspoken preacher for a husband and being involved in the type of work they were.

"Sit down, Mrs. Taylor. I'd hate for anything to happen to you. Your family has already caused me enough problems."

"If you're threatening me, sir, I can assure you that it will do you no good. I kindly remind you that this is my house and you have no right to spew such threats."

"Other than the fact that you have harbored rebel spies?" He turned to Mariah, eyes harsh and calculating. "You lied to me, Miss Taylor. But I reckon it doesn't matter much. It's all turning out better than I could hope."

"Your fight is with me, Amsden. Leave the ladies out of it," Ephraim said through clenched teeth. Amsden's words made him bristle. If he laid one hand on Mariah or Mrs. Taylor ...

"I'm afraid they brought themselves into it when they lied to me."

"They didn't know anything about us coming tonight. They had no say in it."

"Oh, I know they didn't. If they had, you would've never shown. Isn't that right, Miss Taylor?"

Ephraim clenched his fists. The ropes cut into his skin and sent pins and needles through his hands.

Mariah glared, crossing her arms. "I don't know what you're talking about."

"You're a terrible liar," Amsden snarled.

"And you have no manners," she quipped back.

Amsden had moved to the doorway of the adjoining room. He made a sweep of it with his eyes, then rifled through the drawers of the desk, removing a revolver and anything else that would be of use to his prisoners.

Satisfied that he had checked the room thoroughly, he turned to his men. "We'll keep them in here for now. Stay and guard them. We'll be back after we find that little brat and bring him back." He turned to Mariah and Mrs. Taylor. "If you will, grant me your company."

Mrs. Taylor gave him a look Ephraim wouldn't soon forget. Amsden apparently didn't know how cantankerous the Taylor women could be.

Ephraim closed his eyes and leaned his head against the wall after they were left alone in the room they had been concealed in the first time they had come. This day got better by the minute.

"You reckon there's any chance the Taylor boy will find the captain?" Chris broke into his thoughts.

"If Gideon has anything to say about it," Ephraim said.

They had left Gideon outside to tend the horses. He had yet to come in, which meant he was aware of what was happening. Or at least, that's what Ephraim prayed.

"Let's hope they're hightailing it back to camp."

Ephraim glanced around the room, eyes coming to rest on the faulty panel across the room. A smirk played on his lips. "What do you think Amsden would do if we disappeared?"

Confusion clouded Chris' expression, then he followed Ephraim's gaze and a grin lit up his face. "Only one way to find out."

A small flicker of hope was beginning to grow.

Mariah's mind whirled with the events of the evening. If only things had been different. If only they hadn't come back. If only she had been able to warn them away.

Lord, what is your will in all this? You know our cause is just. Will you let innocent men die? Papa is already in prison for smuggling your Holy Scriptures. Will you let Ephraim and Chris suffer too?

The search for Benjamin had thus far turned up no one. She could only hope he was searching for the scouts. If there was any hope of rescue from this nightmare it would be through them. Ephraim had said that Captain Flanagan wasn't one to stand by and let good men die. If ever there was a time for him to prove that, it was now.

She turned her eyes away from the cheerful glowing candles in the window as they approached the house. Those candles. Those betraying candles. How different the night would look if Amsden had never noticed them. Ephraim and Chris would be free.

A shout from the house aroused the attention of all in the yard. "Captain, they're gone!"

Amsden froze momentarily, then flew into action. He stormed up the front steps and into the house. A moment passed before the shouts and curses filled the night air.

"Captain, I will ask you to refrain from such language," Mother rebuked with fire in her eyes.

Captain Amsden was in no mood for a lecture about his language. He barked for his men to search the house and grounds. "Find them," he hissed. "I want them alive. I've a score to settle."

A flurry of boots and swords, rifles and bayonets buzzed through the rooms. Mariah stole a puzzled glance at mother. What had happened in the short time they were gone? If Chris and Ephraim weren't in the house or outside ...

A rush of adrenaline surged through her. Amsden may have made his mistake. Now to hope that no one would discover it. Mother's eyes told Mariah that she too had a good idea of where the missing prisoners were.

They took their seats at the table, waiting for the men to finish their search. Amsden stormed down the stairs, fury blazing from his eyes. "You fool," he bellowed to the soldier. "How could they disappear right under your nose?"

The soldier's face had lost all color and fear found harbor in his eyes. "Sir," he stammered. "I don't know. They were here and then – they weren't."

Amsden swung his pistol as though to strike him. "I can see that."

Mama rose from her chair. "Captain, I will not tolerate you abusing this young man in my home."

Amsden sneered at her. "I will not tolerate whatever shenanigans it is that you are perpetrating here in *your* home. When I find them, I swear I'll kill them. Then how impertinent will you be?"

An out of breath soldier clambered in the door. "Captain, sir, a troop of men coming up the road."

"Ours?"

"Far as I can tell, sir. Looks like Colonel Whipple."

Amsden sheathed his sword and straightened his coat. Then walked out to greet the coming soldiers. Mariah glanced at Mama, waiting for direction on what to do next. She stepped to the doorway, hands clutching the billows of her skirts. Mariah had always remembered her to be a woman of quiet resolve. She had to be, being the wife of a Baptist preacher in the backwoods of Virginia, and now being the wife of a rebel preacher in prison.

The thunder of boots on the ground rumbled louder as the troop approached the house and came to a halt. Voices carried on the wind, making anyone within a distance privy to their conversation.

"What's the meaning of this, Amsden? I told you to see that no word of our movement got through the lines. Not to terrorize rebel women and children."

"Sir, I was ensuring that your orders were carried out. I had reason to believe that Mrs. Taylor and her daughter were engaged in the harboring and abetting of members of the Flanagan Scouts. As it stands, I have indeed captured two of them who I believe were attempting to cross lines to warn the Confederate Army."

Whipple removed his gloves and leaned forward in his saddle. "Where are they?"

At this Amsden's face turned paler than a haint's. Mariah covered her mouth to keep back a laugh. She was enjoying this too much.

"Sir ... they ..." he stammered, helplessly unable to explain the whereabouts of his alleged prisoners.

Whipple tilted his head to the sky, obviously growing impatient with the situation. "Stop prattling like a mad man and tell me where they are, Amsden. You're quickly causing me to question whether a demotion may be in order."

Amsden pulled himself to attention and gazed past his commander. "I don't know, sir. One of my men let them escape."

Whipple slapped his gloves over his knee in fury. "A man's men are only as good as he is, Amsden. If there is any blame, it lies with you." He tugged his gloves back on. "You better pray you find them before they are able to alert the rebels of our offensive, because if they are waiting for us, I will make sure you lead the first charge into their firestorm."

His eyes were filled with fury, and for a fleeting moment Mariah could almost feel sympathy for Amsden. It was short-lived however. She hadn't forgotten all the trouble he had caused them.

Colonel Whipple shouted a command to one of the junior officers with him, who left only to return a short while later. He brought with him a man with hands bound. It was difficult to see in the moonless night, but something about the figure was familiar to Mariah.

Papa. Could it be?

"Is this another of your prisoners, Amsden?"

"Yessir. He is being held for passing contraband on to the rebels." At this Amsden's face glowed with smug satisfaction.

"*Contraband?*" The prisoner asked. Now Mariah knew without a doubt his identity. "Are the Holy Scriptures contraband now?"

Amsden struck out with the flat of his blade. Mariah gasped and Mama's eyes lit up with a silent fear as she watched.

"For the love of all that's good, Amsden. You can capture a shipment of Bibles, but enemy scouts evade you?" He turned to the man beside Papa. "Release him. We haven't the men to waste on babysitting rebel parsons."

Amsden almost seemed to protest his commander's decision, but remained quiet. The soldier slid a knife from its sheath and cut the ropes binding Papa's hands.

This must have been all Amsden could take. "Sir, I encourage you to reconsider. This family is believed to be connected to illegal operations. I have been vehemently working toward uncovering evidence that the *good parson* is involved in more than the holy work of God." Amsden spoke with such hate that Mariah shuddered to listen. Her heart throbbed, waiting, watching for what would be the final say. Papa's expression carried no worry. He tilted his head as he listened to his accuser. She wished she could feel the same sense of peace.

Whipple looked down on Amsden with evident disdain. "Don't you think we ought to be more concerned with the scouts that you let get away?"

He turned his mount and passed the signal for his men to move out. Mariah watched the trail of men move in rhythm with one another, as though they were all part of the same machinery. War machinery. Whatever lay ahead of them was sure to be a baptism of blood and death. She supposed it was her Christian duty to feel remorse for them. But if she was honest, it was hard. She hoped their boys gave the Yankees everything they had. After all, war had never been the Confederacy's desire. The federals were the ones who had raised an army to invade Virginia.

A bed of hot embers couldn't have been more red than Amsden's face. His face twisted in anger. "Get the horses brought around, corporal. We're leaving." Then he turned to Papa. "I assure you this isn't over."

He mounted and spurred his horse into a gallop, his men trailing behind. In the time it took for them to cross the yard to where Papa stood, tears had formed in Mariah's eyes and threatened to spill over. He wrapped his arms around her and Mama tightly, and Mariah squeezed her eyes shut. He was back with them safe and sound for now. She hadn't realized until then that she had been holding her breath as the scene unfolded. Now she released it and deeply breathed in Papa's familiar scent. She wished the moment could've lasted so much longer, but the Yankees were moving and so must they.

Papa started to the house and straight for the hiding place. Mama closed the door and rammed the bolt into its place. "Watch to see that they don't come back," she commanded Mariah. "I wouldn't put it past Amsden."

Then she disappeared into the room with Papa. It was easy to hear the scratchy sound of the fake panel scraping as it was removed. Boots shuffled on the floor, then voices. A moment passed and the foursome emerged from the room. Ephraim was cutting away the rope that held Chris' hands behind him.

"They're marching on Fredericksburg. If they get there before we do ..." Ephraim's voice trailed off. The knife cut through the last of the rope binding Chris. "Do you have any weapons in the house? We happen to have lost ours."

"Yeah," Chris grumbled. "My favorite revolver, and it ends up in the hands of a filthy Yank."

Papa nodded and crossed the width of the room. He dropped to his knees and pried up the edge of one of the floor boards. Mariah gaped as he pulled a pistol from the floor. How had she never known about that spot?

Ephraim shared her surprise. "How many of those hiding places do you have in this house? I'm beginning to wonder if anything is as it seems."

Mama smiled with a twinkle in her eye as Papa handed him the gun. "More than you might imagine."

"We'll take separate routes," Ephraim said to Chris. "If anything happens to one, the other might still get through."

Mariah reached for her shawl hanging on the hook by the door. She was acutely aware of the eyes resting upon her.

"Where do you think you're going," Ephraim asked.

"With you." Her voice sounded much braver than she felt.

"Not on your life, Miss Taylor. The entire county from here to Fredericksburg will be crawling with Yanks."

She turned to Papa. "It only makes sense for me to go. A woman is more likely to make it through the lines. And you've always told me that sometimes we have to sacrifice for something greater than ourselves. Didn't Esther and Jael do the same for their countries?" She was surprised by the sound of her own voice. It could almost be taken as confident — or at least she hoped that was how it was taken. She squared her shoulders back and tried to look more sure of her argument than she felt.

It was evident that Ephraim and Chris were still not convinced. But Papa rubbed the side of his face thoughtfully. She pulled her shawl around her and tied it in the front. "You said yourself what will happen if our troops aren't warned. And someone needs to see that Ma Fletcher makes it out of the city."

Finally Papa nodded. "She's right. She knows the routes like the back of her hand. We can't risk them making it to Fredericksburg unannounced."

"All right," Ephraim finally relinquished. "You'll take the revolver then. Let's get going. It'll already be a miracle if we make it in time. Especially with Amsden and his men looking for us. If the boys return with the scouts — "

"I'll tell them, Sergeant. Now you best be going or Fredericksburg will be in ruins before night falls tomorrow."

Mariah and Chris lead the way out into the frosty night. Pastor Taylor grabbed Ephraim's arm, bringing him to a stop before he could follow.

"Watch out for her, son."

Ephraim nodded. "I promise I will, sir."

They set off in a dead run. Every moment that wasted was one more chance that the Federals would make it to Fredericksburg and take it by surprise.

Ephraim couldn't help but wonder where Gideon and Benjamin were in all this. Amsden would've said something if they had been caught. He was just that nasty as to enjoy waging war against children. He furrowed his brow and braced against the icy wind cutting through him.

A few miles passed beneath them, the thunder of their hooves carrying on the wind. Rounding a corner, Ephraim pulled up sharply on Shenandoah's reins, barely avoiding a collision with a shadowed figure on the path. Chris and Mariah pulled up beside him.

Out of breath and wide eyed like a cornered wildcat, Benjamin froze in terror. Then relief flooded his face as recognition struck him.

"You've got to stop him, Sergeant Bryant! I tried to tell him, but he wouldn't listen."

"Woah, slow down," Ephraim said. "Stop who?"

"Gideon," Benjamin gasped. "He came after me on his horse when I left the farm. Dropped me at camp to find Flanagan, and took off again. Said he was going to warn the army."

Ephraim shot a glance to Chris and Mariah, his heart racing. He didn't like the way this was sounding. "He's headed to Fredericksburg."

Chris released a breath that froze in the air. "We best get going then."

Ephraim nodded and returned his attention to Benjamin. "Get home as fast as you can, but be careful. The Bluedevils are crawling all over tonight."

The boy nodded solemnly and took off.

Mariah and Chris spurred their mounts on, each taking a different route, and Ephraim followed suit. He leaned close to Shenandoah's neck, narrowly missing branches that flashed by. He had to make sure Gideon got out of town safe. Instantly his mind swirled with thoughts too loud to ignore. Gideon was walking into a battle that was shaping up to be one of the worst this war had seen so far. He was just a boy. He had never seen battle up close. His time with the scouts had sheltered him in the confines of courier duties. He had no idea what he was walking into. Ephraim put his spurs in Shenandoah's sides.

If anything happens to him ...

The thought tormented Ephraim. Gideon had a way of grating on him, but the truth was it wasn't his fault. He couldn't help it that he had the same enthusiasm that Sam once had. That his eyes lit up with excitement over the same things Sam's had. Or that the companionship he sought with Ephraim was too painful a reminder of all that had been lost. He was only a boy, soon to become a man by the baptism of battle.

Chapter Ten

Shenandoah tore through the wind. The darkness was both an ally and an enemy. If he was having difficulty seeing, the Yanks were too. Or at least he hoped. It was risky riding through the woods. But it was even more risky taking the road, where they would be moving troops.

Shenandoah's ears laid down in the wind. He could feel her sides heave with heavy breathing. The babble of the river grew louder as they approached its banks. This time of year it was brimming at the edges with the icy water flowing down from the mountains. It would be risky to cross it on horseback, but there wasn't time for anything else. The Federals were on the move, the troops needed to be warned, and Gideon and Mariah would be caught in it all.

Shenandoah only hesitated slightly by the water's edge. Its rushing tide drowned out the noise of the night. He didn't have time to cross at one of the fords. Ephraim patted her neck. "Come on, girl. A lot depends on you getting me across this river."

Lord, you parted the sea for the Israelites to escape pharaoh's army. I'm not asking for anything like that. But I could use a miracle about now.

Deeper they sank into the muddy water. Higher it surged against Shenandoah's legs until finally reaching his own. He grit his teeth against the cold. Hesitation crept over him. One wrong step from Shenandoah and they would both be lost.

They were almost to the middle now. Deeper than he had ever hoped to be in a river in mid-December. The water was approaching his thigh. Suddenly he felt Shenandoah pitch forward, the rolling water growing rapidly closer. He grabbed the saddle horn. She recovered her footing, but it was becoming clearer that they weren't going to make it the way they were now.

He slipped from the saddle, still gripping the reins, and dropped into the ice cold water. The current tugged at him, threatening to take him with it. If they could just make it a little farther, the water would be shallow enough to stand again. He pushed himself to swim harder, faster. Make it just a little farther. The shore grew closer and finally Ephraim could feel the muddy river bottom beneath him. Sopping wet, he clambered onto solid ground again, stopping only for a moment to catch his breath. He pulled himself back into the saddle.

It wasn't long before he passed a house and then another. He had reached the outskirts of town. He breathed a silent sigh of relief. He had made it in time. All was peaceful and quiet. Sleep seemed to hold most of the town in its grip.

Not for much longer.

A sentry ordered him to stop as he approached the area he hoped to find the army. He reigned in Shenandoah. "Sergeant Bryant, Flanagan's Scouts. Is your commander here?"

A thunderous boom shattered the December morning. Then another answered.

It had begun. Ephraim threw a glance over his shoulder toward the river and the battle. Word had reached General Lee a short time before Ephraim had arrived. Whether it had come soon enough would only be revealed by time.

Sharpshooters had taken up places in the buildings close to the river, offering them the opportunity to slow the Union's crossing. Even as he spoke, bridges were being built to usher in the invaders. Ephraim doubted that they would be able to stop them completely, but perhaps they could hold them off long enough for the civilians to evacuate safely. Even now, town had come alive with the precursory panic before a battle. Women hurried down the streets, tugging along wide-eyed children. The sounds of battle scared the smaller ones and tears fell down their cheeks. Others cried inconsolably. An aged, old woman limped slowly, almost overwhelmed by the flow of panicked traffic, carrying a burdensome bundle of belongings.

What had been reminiscent of a still-life painting hours before was now transforming into chaos.

Ephraim winced. This was the shattered reality of war. The clattering thunder of wagon wheels and hoofbeats drew his attention. A driver-less wagon careening down the street approached rapidly, its horses likely startled by the gunfire.

Somewhere in this chaos he would find Gideon. But where? Time wouldn't stand still, and the Yankees were coming. He raced through the panic-stricken streets.

Show me where he is, God. Please show me.

He squinted into the distance, eyes coming to focus on a figure he recognized.

"Gideon!" Ephraim shouted above the noise. His words were instantly whisked away by the roar of cannon fire and rifles. If the young boy had heard him, he showed no evidence of it. He continued his sprint toward the doorway of an old house and ducked in. Ephraim followed, ducking out of the way of fleeing civilians. The house had been abandoned by now, and marksmen had taken up position within its safety. They fired through the windows on the Yankees crossing the river. A thundering boom echoed and shook the foundations of the home. Ephraim covered his head as a framed photograph fell from its place on the wall above him. It hit the floor with a crash. The glass shattered into tiny fragments that scattered over the rug. The faces of a family gazed up at him from the photograph. This was their home, no doubt. Forced to flee from the path the wildfire of war chose to burn. Another explosion shook the building, this time bringing pieces of the ceiling crumbling on top of him. It would be a miracle if they had a home to return to when this battle was over.

Ephraim squinted. A dusty haze hung in the air like fog. He found himself in the sitting room. The fireplace smoldered with the remains of a fire. Its mantle boasted the warmth and festivity of an evergreen garland in honor of the season. In truth, Ephraim had almost forgotten the Christmastide. What peace did life hold? Christmas had ceased its peaceful tidings long ago.

He entered the next room and called Gideon's name again. No response. Then he saw him. Crouched beneath a window. His face had gone as pale as the frost, and terror found refuge in his eyes. Ephraim followed his gaze to the slumped body beside him—that of a sharpshooter. A spattering of blood painted the soldier's face. Gideon was gazing as though his eyes were frozen in place, unable to move away from the horrible scene before him.

"Dead," he whispered. The youthful innocence in his voice had been broken by the harsh truth of war. Ephraim winced, moving to kneel beside him. He reached for the man and checked for a pulse. There was none. The start of the casualties had begun. Where it would end was something known but to the Almighty.

"Come on. Let's get you out of the city while we still can."

Gideon lifted his eyes and anger flashed in them. "I came to warn them. But no one would listen to me."

Ephraim took his arm and helped him to his feet. "You should've done what I told you. You'll never be a scout unless you can learn to resign yourself to the orders you're given." He let out a breath, reining in his own temper that wanted to flare. "But it doesn't matter now. There isn't a soul within ten miles of here that doesn't know they're coming."

Artillery fire rattled the windows again. This time closer than before. Ephraim pushed Gideon toward the back of the house. The farther he could get him from the fighting, the better. The last thing he wanted on his conscience was for anything to happen to Gideon.

Once clear of the house, Ephraim paused to get his bearings. If they followed the street to the left it would take them out of the city — or at least he thought. But Mariah had said she was going to warn Ma Fletcher. His next priority was to find them and see that they left safely.

"Excuse me, sir," he called to a passerby. The man was beyond age for military service and he walked with a limp. He paused and eyed Ephraim questioningly.

"Well? What is it?"

"Do you know where I can find the Fletcher residence?"

"*Ma* Fletcher's?"

"Yes, sir."

He lifted his walking stick and pointed it up a side street. "Three blocks over. A small house with a garden out front."

"Obliged," Ephraim called over his shoulder, already on his way in the direction the man gave.

"I thought you said we were leaving the city?" Gideon hadn't lost his one million questions Ephraim could see.

"*I'm* not. You are. But first we have to find Miss Taylor."

A smirk played over Gideon's face. "Is Miss Taylor going to be your sweetheart?"

Ephraim's heart picked up pace and he rubbed his forehead. Was it so obvious to *everyone*? It would be a lie to say that he hadn't grown fond of her — no matter how hard he had tried not to.

He looked over his shoulder at the sound of footsteps pounding the ground. Three soldiers approached, running vehemently toward the growing sound of battle. Ephraim grabbed Gideon and pulled him out of the way. They were getting closer to the fighting. "Stay near me," Ephraim shouted above the noise.

Gideon nodded. They turned the street corner and Ephraim nearly tripped over Gideon when he froze stock still. The bridges had reached the middle of the river by now. Federal soldiers continued work amid the hail of fire they were taking. Ephraim saw one thrown from the floating structure with the force of a mini ball and splash into the icy water. Another man was sent to take his place and the work continued.

He moved in front of Gideon to block the sight with his body. The boy had already looked death in the eye once. His young eyes didn't need to see war's horrors so closely. A crash sounded in their ears as a cannon fired toward the building they were in front of. The concussive wave brought them to the ground. Pain racked Ephraim's body as he slammed into the frozen ground. His vision went black and a persistent ringing in his ears drowned out all other sounds. He groaned and pushed off the ground with his hands as vision slowly returned. The artillery was getting too close for comfort. The sooner he could get everyone out was for the better.

As the edges of his vision returned a hail of rifle fire came down around him. The Yanks had caught sight of them and were doing some target practice. Finding a sudden burst of motivation, he scrambled to his feet, searching for Gideon. A pit formed in his stomach as his eyes fell on the boy.

No. No, God, not Gideon. He's just a boy.

He half-tripped-half-slid beside him and scooped him into his arms. His shirt was torn revealing bloodied flesh, rank with new blood that spurted from his stomach in pulses. From a gash above his left eye more blood poured. His eyes were closed as though he was asleep. Ephraim hugged him closer to his chest and stumbled over the remains of the building. A sharp protruding edge of brick tore his pant leg and knee upon contact. Dust filled the air, causing a violent coughing fit. More artillery reigned down over the area. He could hear their own boys answering back.

Lord, have mercy. Will there be anything left by day's end?

Somehow he forced himself to run until they were out of range of the guns. Only then did he gently lay Gideon down to assess his injuries. He was no surgeon but he had seen enough of battle and wounds to know that Gideon was teetering on the brink of death. If the bleeding didn't stop soon, he would be gone before infection ever even posed a threat. A hot tear threatened at the corner of his eye. Life's injustice never ceased to reopen the wounds of the past. His family had died with not a thing he could do to stop it. So would Gideon.

He pushed away the emotions and thoughts, burying them in the deepest part of his heart. Gideon was only another casualty of the war. He was nothing so special as to warrant the brokenness that came so easily from within Ephraim. Ephraim didn't want a family. There was no room in this life for the pain it caused. Gideon meant nothing to him. Nothing. Now if only he could convince himself of it.

He lifted him to his chest again and pressed forward into the hazy scene unfolding. Just a block or two more and they would find Mariah.

If she made it through the lines all right.

She had to have made it through. She had to. He had made a promise to Pastor Taylor that he intended on keeping. The final steps of the way seemed to drag on for eternity. His lungs were starved for oxygen after breathing the smokey air. He was acutely aware of Gideon's increasingly shallow breath. At last he arrived at the home described to him by the stranger. He recognized the horse, tied in front of the house. Mariah had made it. He climbed the stairs to the house and used his boot to knock loudly.

"Miss Taylor," he shouted. A flurry of sounds and hushed whispers came from within before finally the door swung open. Mariah stood before him, her face flush with worry. The fire in her eyes that had become so familiar exploded into a blaze as she gazed down to the small body he carried.

"Have mercy," she whispered. Then composure took over in her voice and she stepped aside to allow him entrance. He brushed past and laid Gideon on the sofa. Mariah and Ma Fletcher hovered over him. They worked as though they had seen a thousand young boys marred by battle.

"He needs a surgeon," Mariah said. She laid her hand on his forehead tenderly, brushing away the blood and sweat that had started to bead.

Ephraim nodded. "First we need to get all of you out of the city. It won't be long before all of this will be turned into rubble. Heaven help whoever is left."

"Leave the city? *I'm* not leaving," Ma Fletcher said.

Ephraim sucked in a breath. He admired her spirit, but there wasn't time for him to argue with her. "The Yankees are crossing the river. This town will be a battlefield soon."

She pursed her lips and planted a hand on her hip. "You think I can't hear the cannons for myself?" She squinted her eyes and looked him up and down.

"No, ma'am, but—"

She took his arm with a hand gnarled by a life of hard work. "This is my home. My children were born here. My husband is buried in that graveyard yonder, and I intend to rest beside him when the good Lord calls me. I ain't about to let no Lincolnites rob me of that. If you really would do good by an old woman, stop them Yankees in their tracks."

Ephraim grit his teeth. The protector inside of him wanted to beg her to leave. In a few more hours it would be near impossible for a living soul to remain unharmed in this city. But another portion of him understood her refusal to go. It was the very thing they were fighting for — the freedom to live unhindered by a government that wished to control every detail from the cradle to the grave. How could he ask her to give it all up?

"Go on now, get. Don't you have more pressing matters than to stand here watching out for an old woman?"

Mariah spoke now. "We aren't going to leave you here. It's madness. The Yankees will have no mercy on the city." Urgency found a home in her voice.

Ephraim nodded. "I'm sorry, ma'am. But I have to insist you leave with Mariah."

Ephraim scooped Gideon up once more. His body was so small and helpless. He had been a nuisance more than once, it was true. But Ephraim couldn't bear the thought of losing him.

He led the way back into the crowded street, Mariah directly beside him, fussing over Gideon. Ma Fletcher paused briefly for a final look at her home. Sorrow overflowed the banks of her soul and poured from her eyes. War was indeed a terrible thing.

Ephraim looked up the street. A wagon with a young boy driving was heading with the flow of civilians fleeing. He called to them and they came to a halt. "Are you heading out of town?"

A weary looking woman nodded at him from the seat beside the boy. Her eyes fell upon Gideon and didn't move.

"Can I impose upon you to let them come in your wagon? The boy needs a surgeon badly," Ephraim pressed.

She covered her mouth with a handkerchief and a sob wracked her body. "There will be no one left," she cried. "No one left after it all ends. We'll die at their hands."

The team of horses flicked their tails and threw their heads, anxious over the atmosphere. Ephraim glanced around at the increasing rifle fire and war sounds. He didn't have time to deal with a woman crying incoherently. She was obviously beyond distraught by the events of the day.

He nodded to Mariah and Ma Fletcher. "Climb up."

"Wait," Mariah said, turning to gather Tempest's reins and secure them to the wagon. Once finished, she helped Ma Fletcher up before taking refuge in the back of the wagon herself. With painstaking carefulness Ephraim handed Gideon to them, then turned to the boy in the front. "Drive and don't stop until you're well out of the city."

He nodded in earnest, his eyes wide with the weight being thrust on him. Guilt ate at Ephraim's heart with the knowledge that it was indeed much for a young boy to be plagued with. He would take them if it weren't for his being needed in the battle.

"Miss Taylor," he said, hesitating slightly. "Be careful, and see that Gideon isn't left alone." He was conscious of his voice growing husky with emotion, and he looked away.

The boy flicked the reins and the wagon jolted roughly over the cobblestone. Still the wails of his mother filled the air. Ephraim watched for a moment as the distance between them grew larger. What was this feeling inside of him? His heart felt as though it was torn with a hot poker. And for what? For a woman who didn't even like him and a child that had gotten on his nerves more often than not.

God, let them survive. Please don't take them too.

He shook his head and forced the feeling away. He had done what he could for them. Now he had a duty to his country to fulfill.

Chapter Eleven

December's wind carried the sounds of battle with them as they bounced down the rutted old roads leading them to safety. Already smoke was filling the sky above Fredericksburg. It streamed in columns, like ghost hands reaching to the sky. In front of them and behind them fellow refugees wearily tread the dusty trail, fleeing the wrath of the Yankee army.

"When will it end?" Mariah asked with weariness in her voice.

Ma Fletcher only shook her head. Mariah cradled Gideon in her arms, his blood seeping through the layers of clothing until she felt the warm sticky substance against her own skin. She wanted to close her eyes and wake up in another world. One without battle. One where peace abounded rather than the bitterness of war. The sight of Gideon's wounds turned her stomach. Raw and painfully inflamed. She could see the steady pulsing of his blood in the veins left exposed. It would indeed be a miracle if he survived.

"Please, Gideon, live," she whispered close to his ear. Her hand stroked the edge of his cheek in gentle motions, eventually falling into a rhythm with the jolting wagon.

It was all a nightmare that she wished to wake up from. Father's arrest, the attack on Fredericksburg, Gideon's injury, and Sergeant Bryant lost somewhere in the midst of the battle. Another thunderous boom wafted to them on the wind. It sent a chill down her spine and she clasped Gideon to her closer still.

He's only a child, Lord. He can't die. He can't.

But what if he did? Could she trust that God had a plan? Could there still be peace in spite of her circumstances?

A refugee camp had already formed in the hills outside of Fredericksburg. Women and children, old folks and babies, milled about like sheep lost in the wilderness. Some had begun to build temporary shelters. Others seemed at a loss for what to do. A heavy sense of dread hung over the camp.

The first casualties from the battle had already begun to arrive at the field hospital that had been erected. Mariah swung her feet down from the wagon, landing on the partly frozen mud, and searched for someone to help her carry Gideon. "Sir," she called to an older gentleman passing by. "I have a young boy wounded in the battle. Will you help me carry him to the surgeon?"

The man obliged, lifting Gideon with ease. Mariah looked to Ma Fletcher.

"Go on, child. I'll be fine."

Mariah nodded and followed the man into the nearest tent. A slender man with tender eyes hidden behind spectacles met them. His sleeves were rolled up above his elbows and his arms were tinted the crimson color of blood.

"Lay him here," he said, motioning to a table.

The man complied, then left without a word. Mariah watched the doctor anxiously. He felt for Gideon's pulse first. Then examined the wound. "Is he your brother?"

"No, sir. A friend."

"Where are his parents?"

"He hasn't any."

The surgeon nodded. "He's gravely injured, miss. I don't know that there is much I can do for him."

Mariah's stomach churned and her heart leapt. "You *will* try, sir? He's ... only a child."

The surgeon snapped his head up with eyes ablaze. "Of course I will. I only want you to know that it will be some time before you hear from me as to his condition. But I will send for you as soon as I know any more."

Mariah's heart accelerated its rhythm. She had promised Ephraim that she wouldn't leave Gideon.

"Please, sir. I — want to stay. He knows me. I can be a calming presence for him."

He studied her for a moment. Then started into action addressing the wound. "I need level-headed, miss. It will do neither me nor him any good if you break down into hysteria while I work. He's badly hurt and you'll see more blood before you'll see less. Do you think you can resign yourself to that?"

She grit her teeth and clenched her hands at her side. "Sir, I believe I can."

He locked eyes once more. "Fine then. I need you to hold him still."

Gideon had begun to stir. His eyes flickered open. They were a window into his soul. Fear, pain, and confusion all swirled in a muddled mixture within him. "Sergeant Bryant?"

Mariah brushed her hand on his forehead and down his blood-streaked cheek. "It's Miss Taylor. All is going to be well, Gideon. The doctor is going to see to that."

He squirmed under the pressure from the doctor's capable hands. "Where's Sergeant Bryant? Is he all right?"

"Hush now. He's just fine."

Or at least he was when we left him.

Gideon moaned, his lower lip quivering. Whether from fear or pain, Mariah wasn't certain. She focused her gaze on his face. The sight of the doctor working made her stomach do summersaults, and she couldn't let it do that. Gideon deserved to have someone there with him whom he knew and could feel some trust toward.

"I'm going to remove the shrapnel now," the surgeon said. "Would offer him something for the pain, but there is none thanks to the blamed Yankees. Hold him still as best you can."

She nodded and braced herself for what was needed from her. At first the pain must have been bearable. But then Gideon cried out with the most hideous shriek she had ever heard and threw himself forward. Mariah lost her grip on him momentarily.

"Hold him still," the surgeon shouted at her. His voice was gruff and irritated.

"I'm trying," she said.

She leaned over Gideon's body which was quaking uncontrollably. Her voice gently hushed him. It seemed an eternity would have passed quicker. At last it was over and Gideon drifted into unconsciousness. Mariah straightened and wiped her sleeve across her face, beaded with sweat. The surgeon was wiping the blood from some of his instruments.

"Will he live?" she asked hesitantly.

"That's something only the Almighty knows. Time will tell us. But I would prepare for the worst." He motioned for a nearby aid to assist him in moving Gideon from the table.

Once they moved him to his own little cot, Mariah started out to find Ma Fletcher. She found her in a group of women seated around a small fire. Their eyes harbored the worry felt by the entire encampment of refugees.

Ma Fletcher turned her attention to Mariah. "How is he?"

Mariah shrugged, unable to speak the worrisome outlook. Tears threatened to come with every thought that arose.

"Them Yankees are nothing more than devils," a woman said from across the fire. Her eyes blazed with indignation and she gazed at the columns of smoke over the city. "Have they no respect for the lives they have destroyed? What of the little ones who are sleeping in the cold this night?"

A ripple of murmurs chased her words around the fire. Mariah felt it better not to join the conversation. If she opened her mouth now she was afraid of what would come out. It was true. What did the Yankees know of war? It wasn't *their* homeland that was now ravaged by the destruction of shells and bullets. It was not *their* soil that was soaked with the blood of the dead.

"They're human, just as we are. And souls that need the Savior." Ma Fletcher's soft voice prodded her with conviction. "It seems we'd be better suited praying for them."

Mariah rose from her seat and wandered into the field overlooking the destruction of battle. She could see tiny figures running hither and yon like ants scurrying over the ground, waiting to be crushed by the hand of war.

Ma Fletcher was right of course. Being the daughter of a Baptist preacher, Mariah should share the sentiment. It was expected of her. But yet there was something inside of her that warred against it. It was hard to pray for those responsible for so much pain and destruction. Perhaps there were some in their ranks who were good men, only misled. But men like Amsden put a bad taste in her mouth.

She watched light flash from explosions and smoke rise into the sky. Worry clenched her throat. Sergeant Bryant was somewhere out there, no doubt with the other scouts. A shiver ran down her spine. She remembered he had told her that he was prepared for death

— that he even expected to die in this war. She hoped with all that was in her he was wrong.

Lord, be with him. Send your angels to watch over him in this coming fight — with all our soldiers. Give them strength for the battle ahead of them. Grant us victory.

Pandemonium consumed the landscape. Ephraim's heart beat vehemently against his ribcage. For two days the battle had raged. It was an onslaught like he had never seen before. For a time they had fought to keep the town, but now they held their ground in the Heights.

He rested his rifle on the stone wall affording them cover. His sights narrowed on a blue-clad soldier charging toward them. With the release of Ephraim's trigger the man fell, joining the ranks of his fallen comrades.

Ephraim ducked down to reload. How much longer could they withstand the attack? The field was a perfect sea of federal soldiers. They had repelled wave after wave in the course of a few hours, and yet still they came.

"Why don't they sound retreat?" the soldier beside Ephraim asked.

Ephraim sat back up, training his sights on another target. "I don't know."

"It's madness!"

Ephraim couldn't argue with that. It seemed the Yankees had an endless supply of expendable lives with which to carry out the attacks. The shouts of officers echoed through the ranks, partly drowned out by the roar of cannons and rifles. Heavy smoke and dust blotted out the sun. Horses gave hideous whinnies as they fell in the fight.

The whistle of a mini ball buzzed in Ephraim's ear, and the weight of a body slammed into him. A spattering of blood sprayed onto his face. Shock consumed him as he looked down into the lifeless face of the soldier he had been talking with only a moment before.

"*It's madness.*"

Madness indeed. Nothing could make men endure this. Nothing — except freedom and the ones they loved.

So what was it making *him* endure this? Thoughts of the terror in Gideon's face when he had found him in Fredericksburg filled Ephraim's mind. He remembered the fear in Mariah's eyes as the wagon carried them out of the city. And it filled him with determination. The Yankees had to be stopped, or all that would be left of their homeland was the smoldering remains of the homes and firesides it once boasted and women weeping for their dead.

He scrambled out from under the fallen soldier, steeling himself for the next wave to come. If any of them survived, it would be only by the hand of Providence.

The approach of night brought more refugees streaming into the camp and thunderous echoes of battle. So the battle raged. More and more casualties were being brought. Mariah joined some of the other women in assisting the surgeon. The hospital had been moved a little way from the refugee camp into an old country church house that would shelter the wounded better. Its pews and altar were now the beds of a hospital ward.

Blood stained the worn old pews. The cries and moans of the wounded and dying replaced the sounds of worship that once echoed within the walls. Humanity's suffering all but erased the memory of what had once been in the humble church house.

Mariah brushed away a lock of hair from her forehead, no doubt leaving a smear of blood mixed with the ash and soot. Her hands felt almost numb from the night's work. Packing lint into fleshy wounds oozing blood, offering what little comforts could be given to men in torment. A sip of water to soothe a feverish delirium, a soft prayer to comfort a pain-ridden soul taking flight to eternity. It all seemed so futile.

Where was peace in so broken a world? To a nation ravaged by the horrors of it all, could there be rest in any heart?

Near the front of the room, a blood-curdling scream rent the air. Where the pulpit stood, a small area had been sectioned off with a stained old blanket for surgery. Anesthetics were almost more scarce in the Confederacy than Bibles. The Confiscation Acts could be thanked for that. Because of it, many men were sentenced to suffer in agony and anguish of both body and soul.

Mariah squeezed her eyes shut, in an attempt to block out the horrid sounds. When would it end?

She sucked in a deep, bone weary breath and steeled herself for what needed to be done. She lifted the bucket of water from its place beside her and moved from soldier to soldier offering a drink from the dipper. With pining they drank, reviving their spirits if only a little.

"Much beholden, miss," a soldier rasped. Though he couldn't have been much older than twenty, his eyes seemed as though they had seen a thousand years of war. The harsh truth was that wars were fought by the young. And when the fighting faded into the mist of humanity's chronicles, the young would be old before their time.

She herself had only seen nineteen summers. Yet within the last two, she had seen more suffering than in the first seventeen.

A sad smile graced her lips and she nodded in response to the soldier's gratitude. Nothing could be said. A simple task such as giving water to a needy soul was only the least of what could be done.

"*For I was an hungered, and ye gave me meat: I was thirsty, and ye gave me drink: I was a stranger, and ye took me in.*"

This was the work of Christ. Why then was there no peace within her?

She moved to the next pew where a much smaller form lay as still as the Virginia night — Gideon. Mariah knelt beside him. Sweat glistened on his forehead and a deathly pallor caressed his face. Tenderly she brushed back a wave of sandy hair from his forehead.

"Mama," he whispered, lip trembling.

"It's all right, Gideon," Mariah soothed. His words made her cringe. Ephraim had told her his mother was long since gone from this world.

The pain written on his face tore at her heart. She lifted his head with one hand and brought the dipper to his lips. "You'll be just fine."

Mariah returned the tin to the bucket beside her and studied his face. Sleep now cradled him in its comforting embrace. His cheeks were flushed a rosy hue as though he had just been out frolicking in the snow instead of lying wounded in a field hospital.

Lord, he's only a child. Let him live. Watch over him this night.

She tucked the blanket close around him to protect against the cold creeping into the old church house.

The night hours passed slower than molasses through a sieve. Midnight found that the souls of two of the wounded had slipped into eternity. Their bodies were carried to be with the others awaiting burial. Mariah couldn't allow her mind to think of them there — lifeless and pale, stacked like wood outside the church. Somewhere a wife or a mother, a sister or daughter waited anxiously for their return. Would they ever know what happened? Many times the dead were without anything to identify them. They would be buried without a soul they loved to come and weep over their grave.

"Don't let it stay stored within your soul."

Mariah looked up to the voice interrupting her thoughts.

Ma Fletcher followed her gaze to the bodies being carried out. "It's a burden not meant for you to carry."

Silence veiled them. Mariah swallowed back the lump that formed in her throat. "It doesn't seem like I have a choice but to carry it."

It was a bitter truth. She had looked into the eyes of death as it claimed soldier after soldier. She had seen what she never wanted to. This wasn't the life she had planned for herself. This, her nineteenth year, a tender age that was intended to be full of growth and new experiences. She had hoped for what most girls did — a family and a home. Not war and loss. She had no choice but to suffer the unbearable weight.

Ma Fletcher nodded. "The greatest battles *are* often fought within the soul. But the Almighty never intended for us to fight them alone."

Mariah pressed her hand to her eyes. "How can you be so calm — so unmoved by all of this?"

Ma Fletcher's eyes filled with compassion and she rested her hand on Mariah's arm. "Child, life is a series of trials and tempests. If you're waiting for it to send peaceful seas your way, you're bound to be disappointed." She shook her head. "No, peace is not found in what's around you. It's found in *Who's* within you."

Mariah looked back to the hopeless faces around the ward. "You sound like my father."

Ma Fletcher smiled gently. "Maybe it's time you start listening." She waved her hand. "Now go — get some fresh air to clear your head."

Mariah complied, starting toward the door. Maybe the cold wind could carry away her worries. If nothing else it would give a reprieve from the heavy scent of blood that hung in the air.

Her breath formed in puffs of frost, whisked away by the breeze. She turned in the opposite direction of where the bodies had been carried. She didn't want to see them. Didn't want to sort through the emotions of it all. Her mind swam with confusion, her feet ached, and her hands were stiff with dried blood.

Snow crunched beneath her feet as she closed the gap between the church and the rail fence that enclosed it. Sections of it had been destroyed in the fighting, while others still remained unscathed. She perched on the top rail of a section that had thus far escaped the injury of war. She tucked back a wisp of hair that had fallen from its place securely pinned up at the nape of her neck. There was once a day when she would have fought the uphill battle to keep each strand in place. But now she couldn't seem to find that version of herself. She didn't know if she ever would again.

She gazed at the ceiling of stars painted on a backdrop as dark as the night felt. Then something changed. Something was happening. Something unlike anything she had seen before. Her breath caught in her throat.

Chapter Twelve

The sky was alive. Lights burned like fire, blazing a trail through the stars. Was she going insane?

She turned her attention back toward the church to see if anyone else was also seeing it. Already the walking wounded were making their way out of the building to see the strange phenomena lighting up the sky. The only words spoken were in hushed tones of awe and trepidation. Beneath the glowing, streaming banners each soul stood in an array of emotion. Fear, wonder, reverent silence.

The bloody strife of the previous days slipped a little farther away.

Mariah gathered her skirts, hopped to the ground, and brushed past the stream of soldiers. Inside, she made her way directly to the pew where Ma Fletcher tended Gideon.

"Something's happening," she breathed. "Gideon needs to see it."

Ma Fletcher stood wearily, joints no doubt aching from the cold. "What are you talking about, child?"

Mariah released a heavy breath, her heart racing. How was she going to get him outside? She wouldn't be able to do it alone, and Ma Fletcher wouldn't be able to help. Her eyes searched in the dim light until she found an empty litter against the far wall.

"Private, will you help me carry him to see the sky," she called to a soldier near them.

He hesitated, gaze moving from the door to her, then back. His face softened when he saw the small form lying so still on the pew. He nodded, carrying the litter over.

They lifted him gently onto the canvas and tucked his blanket tightly around him.

Gideon opened his eyes and gazed at her questioningly. Contrasted against the paleness of his face lay a soft curl that had fallen over his forehead. Mariah brushed it back. "I want you to see something," she said.

The wind had picked up since she had been outside. It swirled snow across the ground, then kicked it into the air. Gideon's eyes closed and he turned his face toward the protection of the woolen blanket. Mariah nodded for the soldier to set him down just outside.

"Look up," she whispered.

His eyes fluttered open, then widened larger than the gold buttons on his coat. "What is it? Why does the sky look this way?"

Mariah shook her head. Whatever it was, it could only be the Hand of God.

"I've never seen the sky in such a way, Gideon. But perhaps the Almighty is revealing his power to us." Her hand rested tenderly on his shoulder. She watched him silently gaze at the mysterious lights. Around them the moans and murmur of the wounded had fallen still. Where the sound of battle had resonated on the wind, only a hush lingered now. It was as though the snow had silenced the clamor of hardship, if only for a fleeting moment.

Still the smoke from the smoldering remains of battle draped the landscape. It burned hot and acrid in her soul. Peace had no home in war, no refuge in a war-torn soul. Where then had come so pure and still a calm? And why would peace settle over a blood soaked battle field but not in her heart?

"Do you think that maybe this was what it was like for the shepherds when the angels came to tell them about the Christ-child? The sky all lit in wonderful colors and light?"

Mariah snapped her focus back to Gideon "I don't know. Perhaps."

His face fell solemn and a tear was brushed away. Mariah winced. He was so young to be burdened by war.

She looked back to the dancing lights. *"It came upon a midnight clear, that glorious song of old. From angels bending near the earth to touch their harps of gold..."* She squeezed his hand. "Sing with me?"

He nodded and wiped away another hidden tear. *"'Peace on the earth, goodwill to men from heaven's all gracious King. The world in solemn stillness lay to hear the angels sing.'"*

"What is it?" Chris breathed the question that the men all wondered.

Suspended in the heavens, an unearthly glow appeared. At first it was a faint red hue against the dark night sky. But then it turned a deep shade of scarlet, bleeding through the cloak of darkness as though the universe itself had been mortally wounded in battle.

"It can't be good." Armand, another of the scouts, shook his head slowly. "It surely brings the deaths of many good men."

"And how do you know such things?" Chris asked with skepticism.

"A sign like this can only mean something bad. Look how they turn crimson like the blood flowing o'er the ground this night."

Ephraim stepped out of the ring of light cast by the fire, tuning out the conversation. No matter how much he tried, he couldn't take his eyes off the sky. More colors had appeared now. Green, then gold, and fiery crimson moved and pulsed in a mesmerizing vortex. It was as if the heavens were on fire. What *did* it all mean? He didn't believe in omens. He wasn't superstitious. He knew that the phenomena of nature were ordered by the hand of God. But this night, these lights — they were so different from anything he had known before. They sent a chill through him.

Did they hold some connection with the awful battle they had just come through? Was there a greater meaning for this band of ragged soldiers?

He watched as they swirled and danced. Just as he would focus on one streak of light, it would fade away and another would appear much brighter and more alive than the others previously. Suddenly he felt smaller than he ever had before, and the war seemed far away.

"Do you think Armand is right?" Chris asked, walking up behind him.

"That good men will die before this battle is over? Yes. That these lights are a supernatural omen? No." Ephraim could sense the uneasiness in Chris. He was scared. After what they had been through over the past days, who wasn't?

Ephraim could still see the faces of every soldier he saw die. More than he ever wished to see again. Destruction had reigned with its merciless hand.

The night was silent now. A strange calm had settled over everything with the appearance of the ghostly lights. Only occasionally would a shot ring out from a sharpshooter's rifle. Shadowy figures covered the fields – the dead, the wounded, and those praying to survive. He imagined it would all start again tomorrow.

"It's almost Christmas," Chris said more to himself than anyone. "What I wouldn't give to be home." He looked up to the sky wistfully and sighed. "So much for peace and goodwill to men."

"The first Christmas brought a type of peace that can weather even the darkness of this world," he said, still gazing at the dancing lights. "Jesus Christ came to reconcile the sinner to the Savior. And through it, bring hope and rest and peace."

He barely recognized his own voice. Who was he to tell Chris about the peace of God?

"I'm not one to blaspheme the Almighty," Chris said. "Sure seems like if he truly intended to bring peace, though, it would be in a different manner."

"He doesn't often do things in the way we would figure it. There was nothing so conventional about a King being born in a manager. Or the Son of God dying on a cross. But it's the only way the peace of God could enter our hearts."

Chris didn't respond. Ephraim could tell he was thinking about his words though. The silence gave him time to think too. Thoughts of Gideon came easily. He should have never pushed him away. He thought it was for his own good. That's what he told himself anyway. He thought it would be unfair to allow a friendship to form only for Ephraim to be killed in the war. And then there was his own pain to consider. It was painful to think about gaining a family. Just one more thing to lose, destroying everything inside of him again. Mama and Sam had been everything to him. He had dreams of giving them a nice house instead of one that let in the Virginia wind and rain, of having enough food to feast through the long winters, of ...

He shut his eyes tightly against the intrusive thoughts. No use living in what never would be. The past couldn't be changed.

But Gideon ...

Didn't he deserve better than life had given him? If it had been Sam, would Ephraim have pushed him away?

"Remy! Look at me, Remy. I've got your hat. You'll have to promise to give me a ride on your back after chores before I give it to you."

A tear burned its way down his cheek as Samuel's voice echoed in his mind. Memories from a lifetime ago. Christmas 1860. Snow that fell like sugar over the evergreens. A fire glowing in the drafty little house that was home. A young boy, face merry and bright, waiting for the Christmas cakes Mama had promised. Samuel had snatched Ephraim's hat from the peg by the door and held it for ransom, his face aglow with the cheerfulness of the season.

"Sam, let your brother finish his work," Mama had scolded. *"When he comes in, the cakes will be ready and we'll sing carols."*

Chores had never gone so quickly, it seemed, as they did that Christmas night three years prior. The cold didn't sting so much and the work seemed lighter than most days. And the fire never felt so warm as when he came back in, stamping off the muddy, snowy mixture on his boots.

"Remy, can I sit with you?"

"I can't hold my guitar if you're sitting on my lap."

Sam's face had fallen so sincerely sorrowful that Ephraim couldn't tell him no. He could still remember how the boy had scrambled onto his knee and sang at the top of his lungs. They had to have sung just about every carol known to man that night, with the warmth of Christmas, the love of family, and the peace of the Savior consuming them.

"If you could've been there the night of baby Jesus' birth, who would you have liked to be," Sam asked.

Mama hadn't hesitated. *"I'd have been among the shepherds. They were the first to feel the Savior's peace fall over the world and to hear the angels singing. It must've been a glorious sound."*

The sparkle in her eyes could've illuminated the night. That was what he missed the most, what he would give anything to have again.

Morning's early light brought only a ray of hope for Gideon's survival. Life's fragile existence was slipping from his body. Mariah had spent the long night keeping him in as much comfort as she could. The fever ravaging his body stole the life from his face.

She sang carols to him until her voice grew hoarse and he drifted into sleep once more. A night had passed since the strange lights appeared, leaving an unsettling silence when they faded. It had been hours now since she had heard the terrible roar of artillery or blood-curdling screams from the battlefield. Something was surely happening. She hoped and prayed with all her might that the silence didn't mean Fredericksburg had fallen to Union hands.

It wasn't difficult to piece together how terrible the fighting was by looking at the casualties pouring in. Men missing arms and legs, sometimes both. Faces disfigured from a ball or artillery shell. Perhaps what made her heart ache the most was the ones who wept through the night like little children, their souls wounded deeper than any outward injury. She had never seen anything like it. No medicine could remedy and no surgeon could repair the wounds those soldiers bore.

Lord, I'm trying to be still — to rest in who you are. But I feel so restless inside.

Home seemed so far away. Mama and Papa, Benjamin, and Tempest. Had news reached them of all that was happening?

And Ephraim ...

She shivered. The wounds she saw were so bad. Soldiers came in with whole portions of their bodies missing. Their pain and agony would never leave her. She was certain that when she was old and gray she would still see the faces of every soldier she tended in this blood stained ward. She feared, with every new soldier brought in, that it was Ephraim or one of the scouts. Could any of them escape the bloodshed that this battle was perpetrating over the land?

She looked around at the ward. Soldiers with such long faces. They too felt the absence of peace. Heaviness could be felt hanging over them so thick that it threatened to crush their very souls. And this at the Christmastide — a time that should've been filled with the warmth of home and fireside. Of children's laughter, and songs being sung. Of spiced cider and decadent treats only had but once a year.

She blinked back the tears that threatened to spill onto her cheeks. Her hand trembled as she reached over to brush back a feverish curl from Gideon's forehead, picking up with the song they had sung together earlier in the night.

"And with the woes of sin and strife, the world has suffered long; beneath the angel strain has rolled two thousand years of wrong. And man at war with man hears not the love song which they bring. Oh hush the noise, ye men of strife, and hear the angels sing." Her voice grew stronger with the words. They resonated deeply in the aching walls of her heart. Judging from the faces of the men around her, they felt the same.

"Mariah, there are visitors outside looking for you."

Mariah looked up to the sound of Ma Fletcher's voice. She wiped her hands on the makeshift apron covering her skirt. "Me? Are you sure?"

Ma Fletcher nodded. "Said they were looking for Miss Taylor. Don't know of any others here."

She stood and tucked a wisp of hair behind her ear. She quietly moved to the back of the building and stepped out into the daylight, nearly colliding with a tall, gray-clad soldier.

He removed his hat, bringing it to rest in front of him. "Your voice is suited for singing, Miss Taylor."

"Sergeant Bryant," she said in surprise, heat flushing her face at his words. It seemed to be her eternal lot in life to find herself in awkward situations, and of late they seemed to predominately involve him. "I didn't expect you." She nodded to Chris, who stood beside Ephraim quietly.

Ephraim's gaze shifted away from her eyes and he tilted his head slightly, furrowing his brow. "Are you all right?"

"Yes. Why do you ask?" She crossed her arms and raised an eyebrow. "Do I look pale again?"

He brought his hand up partially to his cheek, eyes still filled with concern. "Your ... face," he said, rather awkwardly. "It's bleeding."

Embarrassment flooded her. She knew she had to be an unkempt sight. Her clothing was soiled with blood, vomit, and mud. Her hair was in need of being combed and re-braided. And though she hadn't seen herself in a mirror, she felt certain that dark, weary circles hung beneath her eyes.

She looked away, brushing her sleeve over her cheek. Indignity filled her words. "I haven't had the time to care for my appearance, sergeant. I've slept less than eight hours over the course of these awful days, and I don't need any remarks from you regarding the way I look."

To her surprise, he didn't seem phased by her explanation. He reached into his pocket and pulled out a kerchief. "I only meant to make sure you were uninjured."

Her heart skipped a beat. He cared if she was injured? With another blush she accepted the kerchief offered and turned to the barrel of water beside the tent. She lifted the dipper and poured it over the kerchief, saturating the fabric. With her back still turned, she washed her face with the cloth.

"What is it you needed me for?"

"Our orders are to return with the Captain — "

"And you want to see Gideon before you go." Mariah finished for him.

He ran a hand through the dark shock of hair usually hidden beneath his hat. "Miss Taylor, do you have some aversion to letting me finish a sentence?"

She dried her hands on the apron around her waist and looked up toward the sky, chest rising with a slow breath.

Why must you always be so impatient?

Ephraim shifted his weight from one leg to the other. "Yes, we would like to see him."

Mariah chewed her lower lip. Of course he had come to see Gideon. What other reason would have brought him? He had made it quite clear that he was a soldier and a scout, and nothing more.

She turned to open the door. "I'll take you to him."

The hinges of the old door groaned in protest as she pulled it open. It was quiet now in the ward, thoughts of Christmas and home still lingering. She pressed forward into the conglomeration of beds on the floor, pews, and altar. It was near impossible to keep one's hem from becoming soiled, and she had given up trying. Even the floor boards were stained the color of blood, and her shoes stuck to them with each step. She looked back to Ephraim and Chris. Their faces were heavy, and their eyes lingered on the suffering around them. She could empathize with the emotion that overwhelmed their usually hardened dispositions.

As they approached the pew where Gideon lay, embraced by a feverish incoherency, Mariah stepped aside. Ephraim sank to his knees slowly, as if any sudden movement would steal Gideon away from him. Absentmindedly he dropped his hat beside him on the floor, gaze never leaving the boy. Chris also crouched down to be level with the makeshift bed.

"How is he?" Ephraim's voice was quiet. And for the first time since knowing him, Mariah recognized fear in his words. It was a part of him that she hadn't seen before. Certainly not with regard to Gideon.

"The surgeon said it's hard to tell yet. If we can bring his fever down, he'll have a much better chance for recovery," she said softly.

Ephraim bowed his head, resting it in his hands. Was he praying? She looked to Chris. He too seemed taken back by his words and demeanor. They stepped back to offer him privacy.

"He's usually so ..."

"Bullheaded," Chris offered, eyes still focused on Ephraim. "He's a master at hiding his emotions. He cares about you all a lot more than you might think, Miss Taylor."

Mariah lifted her gaze to him. Though she said nothing, Chris must have known the questions that swirled inside her. He heaved a sigh. "I shouldn't say anything. Ephraim will have my hide if he finds out. But do you remember the day you went to see your father, and Ephraim met you on the road outside town?"

Mariah nodded, even more puzzled now. "He sent me back on Shenandoah and said he had to talk to Captain Flanagan."

"He asked Flanagan to plan a rescue. Nearly begged him to do something. Never seen him so adamant," Chris said, and shook his head. "That's how I know. He cares about your family."

Mariah searched for something to say, but came up empty handed. What *could* be said? She looked over her shoulder and forced a smile as Ma Fletcher approached. It was for the best that she hadn't been there to hear Chris' words.

A moment passed without a word said among them, then two. When Ephraim finally lifted his head again, Mariah could see the streaks on his face where tears ran down through the dirt and gunpowder.

His face quickly hardened again with resolve. Standing to his feet, he approached where they stood. "We came to offer you our escort back home, to see you make it safely. The battle is as good as over."

Mariah stared blankly back at him.

Home.

It seemed that a lifetime had passed since she had left. Indeed, she had seen enough of war and battle to make it feel as though she had aged a hundred years. Through the darkest hours of the past days she had been only focused on the task at hand. But now that the guns had fallen silent for a time, a yearning homesickness flooded her.

She was weary and tired, and the safety and security of home sounded like a dream too good to be true. She looked down to Gideon. She couldn't leave him here alone without a soul he knew. But Ephraim and Chris were here now, offering to take her home. Home to be with Papa and Mama again. And Benjamin — she wondered if he had made it back all right. Her mind swirled with each thought.

Chapter Thirteen

"I wouldn't feel right leaving Gideon alone here. He won't be of use to the scouts or military for some time. And he has a better chance for living if he doesn't remain among all this death and sickness. I want to take him home with me. I'll speak to the surgeon about it, but I'm certain he'll agree that it would be in Gideon's best interest to be free from the dangers of the hospital."

"What would your parents say?" Chris asked.

"I know they would want me to bring him home," Mariah assured. "Mama knows how to doctor better than most of these surgeons. She used to do a lot of it when Papa was a circuit rider. He'll be well tended."

Ephraim stayed silent. She keenly felt his gaze.

"We'll leave tomorrow," he finally said.

Mariah nodded and turned to Ma Fletcher. "We'll be ready."

The elderly woman shook her head. "I can't go with you, child."

Mariah started to argue, but Ephraim spoke first. "Where will you go then? We may have kept the city, but it's in ruins. Half the buildings that were once there are in shambles on the ground. It'll take years to rebuild."

Ma Fletcher's eyes were weary, yet somehow serene. "And what difference does victory make if no one returns to do just that? The bloodshed will have been for nothing. No, I can't just leave my home." She motioned to the wounded soldiers around them. "Someone has to return, rebuild what the Yankees destroyed. For these boys here, if for nothing else."

Dawn scattered its glow across the landscape as Ephraim brought the wagon to a stop outside the old church. He had managed to secure it for use in taking Mariah and Gideon home. Shenandoah and Tempest trotted behind, content for the chance to be free of their riders.

He jumped down from the seat and removed his hat as he entered the sacred building. His eyes searched the dim lit room until they fell on the familiar face he was looking for. Mariah was bent over a wounded soldier, her eyes closed and lips moving. Her soft voice could just barely be heard rising above the low moans of the men. She was praying for the man.

Ephraim lowered his head. He could see that though she had inherited Pastor Taylor's fierceness, she also carried her mother's gentle tenderheartedness.

She lifted a dipper of water and slowly tipped it back for the soldier to drink. Ephraim cocked his head as he watched. Her hands — they were raw and red from her work, and blood stained them. She could've been home, safe and free from the horrors of battle. But she had chosen, insisted even, on coming. Pastor Taylor could be proud of her for that. She loved her country, and there was no denying it.

She had finished with the soldier now and was coming toward him. Though not a full smile, the corners of her mouth turned up gently and her eyes had a light in them not present the night before. Ephraim caught himself nearly smiling back, but stopped short. She was still only part of his duty, and no doubt her feelings for him remained the same as they did the day they met in her barn.

"Are you ready to leave?"

She nodded. "We can't arrive home soon enough for my liking. The surgeon has checked on Gideon for the final time and sent me with instructions until we can get him under the care of a doctor back home."

Ephraim felt uneasy about moving Gideon so long a distance. He was still so pale and weak with the fever. But Mariah was adamant that her folks would insist he come, and his time spent under their roof had left no reason to doubt her. If Mrs. Taylor had any say in Gideon's future, she would have him tucked safely away in their little home as far from battle and war as possible.

"He's too young for soldiering," she had told him once.

He was inclined to agree.

Still, he worried about his ability to survive such a journey. What if it was too much for him? But then, what if he stayed here and contracted something far worse than what he already suffered? Ephraim would never, could never, leave Sam in such a place to die alone. He couldn't leave Gideon to such a fate either.

With the help of a fellow soldier, Ephraim lifted Gideon into the covered bed of the wagon. He moaned and gave a whimpered cry that stabbed Ephraim's heart. Ephraim knelt beside him on the wagon boards, lingering a moment after the soldier who had aided him left.

"I'm sorry, Gideon," he whispered. "I'm sorry for letting this happen to you."

He was just a kid, and Ephraim had let him down. For that he would never forgive himself. He tucked the blanket around Gideon's frail form, and climbed down.

Mariah had finished saying goodbye to Ma Fletcher and stood waiting outside the wagon with Chris, who had just ridden up.

Ephraim extended his hand to help her climb into the wagon. She gathered her skirts and found a foothold on the wagon box, stepping with caution.

After making sure she was settled, Ephraim turned the corner to climb into the front. Chris raised his eyebrows. "So you do have *some* manners about you."

Ephraim pressed his lips into a tight line and gave Chris a shove. "I don't need any remarks from you."

The wagon jolted forward, passing through the sorrowful camp of refugees. Many were beginning to go back to their homes — if they were still standing. Even from a distance, Mariah could see how badly Fredericksburg had been impacted by the battle. She wondered if it would ever rebuild to what it had been before.

She wondered if *they* ever would. Their souls that were marred with the shock of battle — would they ever be the same as they were when they had come to Fredericksburg? She didn't see how they could be.

How vastly different their group was. Ephraim, Chris, and her. How much they had changed in the short time since traveling this road to Fredericksburg. She knew how she herself was changed by it. And though neither Ephraim or Chris had spoken a word about the battle, she could tell from their silence they too were fighting unseen demons. They had seen the cannons, the blood, the shouts and screams. The "heat of battle" she supposed was the title given to what they had endured.

She had seen the aftermath — when the heat of battle had died away, and loss consumed the flame of hope. The terrible sound of the surgeon's saw on human bone, the screams of the poor souls enduring it. It didn't matter that each of them had been in different areas of the battle. Each bore the haunting pain just the same.

She looked up to the opening where Ephraim kept his vigil. His coat blended with the watercolor gray sky and the wind that seemed to wail for the many southern sons lost on Virginia's blood soaked soil. Ahead of them she could see Chris on his mount and the silhouette of his rifle. A yawn overwhelmed her.

Ephraim glanced back at her. "Might as well get some sleep," he said.

She shook her head. She would sleep later. Gideon might wake up and need her. "I'm all right. Besides, we'll be crossing the lines soon and it might be best if I'm not sleeping."

He looked back once more. "I promised your father that I'd see you were taken care of. I'm not about to break my word. You have nothing to fear in that regard." He met her eyes, as though ensuring she heard him, then turned back to the road ahead.

Mariah pulled her shawl tighter around her, heat flushing her face. She hadn't intended to imply that she thought they were incapable of protecting her and Gideon. After all, they were the ones who had watched out for them while Papa was gone. She had no doubt that they would see she made it home unharmed. But she couldn't let herself sleep.

"Thank you," she said quietly. "But I think I'll keep awake, just the same."

He made no reply. Only leaned forward to casually rest his elbows on his knees. A few minutes passed, then he began to whistle a tune, low and clear. It was the carol she had sung to Gideon — the one he had overheard. She blinked back at him. He whistled its peaceful notes for a few minutes before pausing.

"There's a verse of that song I heard once," he said. "Goes like this."

His voice was low, and it mixed with the wail of the wind to create a choir.

"And ye beneath life's crushing load whose forms are bending low,

Who toil along the winding path with painful steps and slow,

Look now, for glad and golden hours come swiftly on the wing,

Oh rest beside the weary road and hear the angels sing.

His voice trailed off, leaving the notes to melt away. "Sometimes you have to rest beside the road, Miss Taylor."

He didn't move his eyes off the road as he spoke. Just stayed stock still and somber. His words echoed in Mariah's mind.

Sometimes you have to rest beside the road.

She leaned her head against the side of the wagon bed and closed her eyes. Maybe she could allow herself to rest a moment. She was safe, and would soon be home.

Ephraim glanced back again into the shelter of the wagon's covering. Gideon lay as still as death itself, the color still absent from his face. But his breathing had grown easier and less labored, which Ephraim took as an answer to his prayers. Beside him, Mariah had finally given up the fight to keep awake. For that he was glad. She needed sleep. Heaven only knew what horrors she had seen in the hospital. He knew from experience that war's cruel images were enough to give even a battle-hardened soldier haunting nightmares.

If you would, Lord, spare her that pain. Don't let her relive all the suffering she has seen.

"And, Lord," he added, with another glance to Gideon. "Help me keep them safe."

Chris signaled to him from up ahead. They were close to the border now. They could only hope the Yanks were preoccupied licking their wounds from the loss at Fredericksburg. He flicked the reins lightly and pulled the collar of his outer coat higher. It was beginning to snow.

He wouldn't mind so much if it was just him. But he had Mariah and Gideon to watch out for. He looked back one more time to ensure they were both all right. Gideon was nestled under as many blankets as they had been able to gather, protected from the harsh cold. Mariah still slept soundly beside him. That was of some relief to Ephraim.

The wagon jolted along through the wooded landscape. Chris would ride ahead for a piece, then return to let them know all was well. All was quiet for some time, but that didn't last.

"Woah up there," the voice called. Soldiers emerged from their hidden place among the trees. They were clad in heavy woolen coats dyed a deep blue. Their eyes were shaded by the brims of their kepis, and rifles resided in their hands.

Ephraim felt for his revolver, securely held in his belt. How Chris had managed to slip past the men unnoticed, he didn't know. But there was no way he would be able to outrun them in a wagon. And if he could, the jolting ride would no doubt kill Gideon. He pulled back the reins.

"Who are you, and what business do you have in these parts?"

Before Ephraim could answer, the other soldier flipped back the canvas covering the wagon. Ephraim bristled and his eyes narrowed, watching the soldier like a hawk. He would protect Gideon and Mariah with his life if need be.

"Look," he said, "they're no threat to you. I'm taking them home."

The soldier cast a suspicious gaze over Ephraim's charges. He looked from them to Ephraim and back again. "What's wrong with the boy?"

"Sick. Might not make it to morning."

It wasn't a lie. Truth was he didn't know if Gideon would survive. They didn't need to know he had been wounded while warning the Confederates of the Fredericksburg attack.

The soldiers' faces softened at mention of Gideon's ailment, but soon resumed their suspicious nature. "And what of you? You're of age to be serving. Question is, on which side?"

Ephraim weighed his options internally. Lying to them wouldn't do much good. They would figure out which side he fought for soon enough. He wore Confederate gray beneath his outer coat.

He looked directly to the one who had spoken first. "I don't think I need to answer that. You've likely got a good idea of which side I take."

The other soldier raised his rifle higher.

Ephraim could see he wasn't impressed. He kept his tone steady. "It's nearly Christmas," he said. "There'll be plenty of fighting for a good while to come. But Christmas ..." He looked over his shoulder to Mariah and Gideon. "They should be home for Christmas."

He held his breath, waiting for a response. It was plain on their faces that they were weighing their decision. Weariness clouded their eyes, much like all the soldiers Ephraim had seen over the course of the previous week. War was wearing them down, and they couldn't help but long for the peace of the season. That much was shared by the men of both armies.

The soldier hesitated a moment, then slowly lowered his rifle. "Can't fault a man for seeing his family safely escorted home."

Ephraim felt his heart pang with an unknown emotion at the mention of having a family. They *weren't* his family. He didn't *want* a family.

The soldier continued on. "I reckon no one needs to know we ever met tonight. Consider it my part of peace and goodwill to men."

He looked to his counterpart, as though awaiting his approval, which he soon gained through a nod.

"Get on then," he barked at Ephraim. "Another day and I suppose we might be killing each other."

Ephraim flicked the reins over the team's back and the wagon began to creak forward. He didn't want to wait long enough for them to change their minds.

"Johnny!" The soldier's voice called after him.

Ephraim looked over his shoulder in time to catch a small pouch that the soldier threw him. He opened it just enough to reveal its contents, then looked back at the man in surprise.

"Merry Christmas," the soldier said, a twinkle in his eyes.

A flurry of voices crept into the dreams that filled Mariah's sleep. But instead of the shouts and groans of the wounded and dying, she heard Mama and Papa's voices.

She sat up, blinking back the sleep from her eyes. The canopy of the wagon swayed back and forth with the wind that howled. From the opening in the back she could see the snow coming down heavier than she ever remembered it to have graced this portion of Virginia. Then a tall imposing figure stepped into the hazy light.

"Papa," she exclaimed, throwing her arms around him in a hug. He lifted her down from the wagon and for a moment she was a little girl again, lost in the peace of another world.

She stepped back, turning to the wagon again. Ephraim and Chris had already lifted Gideon from its protection.

"Bring him inside," Mama said, hurrying to open the door.

Mariah followed closely, keeping the blanket tucked tightly around his neck and face. Mama directed them to lay him on their bed in the side room. She rested her hand on his forehead, worry creasing her brow.

"Hotter than a foundry," she said, looking up at the group gathered around the boy. "Bring a bowl of water."

Mariah nodded and turned to retrieve some from the kitchen. By the time she returned Mama had removed the bloody bandage around his abdomen and was wrapping a clean dry one in its place. She set the bowl on the small table near the bed.

Chapter Fourteen

Ephraim clenched his jaw, moving to the door and the fresh air he needed so badly. Mariah and Mrs. Taylor were tending to Gideon and there was nothing more he could do for the boy. He needed some time to sort through the emotions that had been building for so long.

The sky was a bleak blue-gray color that reminded him of the sea of soldiers, from both sides, that had clashed on the fields below the heights of Fredericksburg. So much bloodshed and life lost to war and its insatiable hunger.

"It was real bad, wasn't it?" Pastor Taylor's voice broke into his thoughts, understanding and strong.

Ephraim gripped the porch rail tightly and nodded, the scenes returning with vengeance. "One of the bloodiest I've seen."

Pastor Taylor turned and directed his eyes to the snow covered evergreens surrounding the house. "I didn't mean the battle, son."

Confusion swept Ephraim's mind. If not the battle, then what was he referring too? "I don't understand, sir."

"When you lost your family."

Silence flooded the moment. How could so much pain be contained in one person's heart? And yet it was the burden he had borne for years now.

"I don't remember telling you about them."

"Mrs. Taylor mentioned it to me." He turned to face Ephraim, eyes softening some. "She's taken a liking to you. Told me about how you boys have seen to it they've been taken care of while I was gone."

Ephraim shrugged. "It wasn't anything, sir. Just doing our duty, like any man worth his salt would do."

Another short span of time passed without a word. Then he spoke again. "Was it one of the epidemics that took them?"

Ephraim nodded, eyes shut against the memory. "Smallpox. I didn't even know they were sick. Got a letter from Mama while I was at the Institute, telling me to come home. She said that my little brother, Sam, wasn't long for this life."

His heart increased its rhythm. Heat flushed his face. The scene before him began to blur with the hot tears spilling over onto his cheeks. "Have you ever seen how quickly smallpox moves, sir?"

Pastor Taylor didn't answer, let him continue unhindered, as though he knew that this was what Ephraim needed.

"I did. I saw. Got my leave and rode through the night to get home for them." A quiver shook his voice and body. "Mama was gone when I got there. She'd come down with it shortly after she sent for me. Gone. I never got to tell her goodbye." A deep well of emotion tore through him. He struggled to keep the tears from coming.

A fatherly hand rested on his back. "And Sam?"

"Sam ..." Ephraim let his gaze go as distant as his mind felt. "Sam hung on. Just long enough for me to come to him. But there wasn't anything I could do for him. I tried, Pastor. I tried. I would've given my own life for them."

Pastor Taylor pulled him into the embrace of a father. "I think they knew that, son. You're a good man. They knew you loved them."

"Have you ever held a tiny body, so lifeless and helpless?" Ephraim choked. A lump rose in his throat.

"Remy, I'm afraid to go alone."

Sam's words had almost shattered Ephraim's heart irreparably. Death had taken his little Sam quickly.

"Don't be afraid. You won't be alone. The angels will come to carry you to Heaven."

"Like they came to the shepherds when Christ was born?"

"Yes, Sam. They'll come for you, and take you to see Jesus. Just like they told the shepherds where they could find him all those years ago."

"I held him all that night, Pastor Taylor. He was so sick. Died Christmas morning," he said through a quivering voice. "Life isn't just. I know that. But isn't it reasonable that I be allowed to grieve that? I don't want a family. God took the only one I wanted. I don't want to ever go through that again."

"It's never wise to let fear rob us of the blessings God intends for us to have, son. I think whether you are willing to admit it or not, Gideon has found a special place in your heart. A place that you feel is betraying Sam. And on top of the guilt, you're scared to lose him like you did your family."

Guilt pricked at his heart. How did Pastor Taylor know so much about him? He had tried so hard to hide any emotion far away. But somehow he saw.

"I never asked God for this."

Pastor Taylor smiled reassuringly. "God has a way of knowing what is best for us before we do. The Lord giveth and He taketh away." He looked up to the night sky once more. "I remember a Christmas once, long ago, when he gave the most precious gift ever known to mankind and placed it in the arms of a young mother. But then the day came when he took that gift from her, because he knew that it was the only way salvation could reach the hearts of man." He leaned heavily against the rail. "I've often thought about the peace that Mary must have felt that first Christmas, holding The Prince of Peace, only for the day to come when he was taken from her in a cruel way with nothing she could do to stop it. It must have seemed terribly unjust to be given something only for it to be taken away. But I think Mary still felt the peace of Christ on the day He died, just like when she held him that very first Christmas."

Pastor Taylor patted Ephraim's back and disappeared into the house again, his words still echoing.

It made Ephraim mad. Probably because it was all true. He'd be lying to say that he hadn't grown to care about Gideon — about all of them. Sure it was never his intention. But the fact was he had. And now he had a decision to make. Could he open his heart to the possibility of a family again?

A twinge of pain stabbed him. Or perhaps it was doubt — doubt that told him he didn't want to love anyone or anything ever again.

But louder yet was the whisper that told him he couldn't stop caring for the Taylors and Gideon even if he tried. Even if he wanted to.

God has a way of knowing what is best for us before we do. The Lord giveth and He taketh away.

He dropped his head, eyes shut against the brisk wind, uncertain if he could find the strength needed within him.

All that week Ephraim couldn't keep his mind off the Taylors and Gideon. The scouts were laying low for a while, being as the Yanks were still riled from their defeat at Fredericksburg. He was going insane with nothing to do and no news of how the Taylors were doing.

And Mariah ... he would be lying to say he wasn't wanting for her company. The first time they had met he had found her to be quite beautiful — any man in his right mind couldn't help but notice it. But the time spent with her had revealed that his attraction went beyond her outward appearances. She was feisty enough to keep him on his toes, but gentle enough to make him want to protect her from all the harm in the world. She had eyes of fire and a heart of gold.

But he wasn't at all sure she shared his sentiment. And then there was Pastor Taylor. He would have to give his blessing to any future relationship of course. Not to mention still the old doubts and fears crept in that told him relationships only brought pain. Did he want to invite that into his life again? That was what he had joined the scouts hoping to avoid.

He stamped his boots and rubbed his hands together, tilting his head to the icy gray sky. He couldn't remember a winter so cold. Footfall behind him brought his attention to where Chris approached.

"Things have been awful quiet today," he said. "I guess that's fitting, what with it being Christmas Eve. Mankind has brought enough bloodshed already. The least we can do is resign ourselves to peace for a time."

Oh hush the noise ye men of strife, and hear the angels sing.

Chris' words brought back Mariah's clear sweet voice singing the old familiar carol. He slipped his hand into his pocket and pulled out the small drawstring pouch given him by the Yankee picket they had come across. He dumped its contents into his hand, revealing an assortment of candies near impossible to find in Virginia now. Ephraim imagined they had likely been the soldier's Christmas gift from home.

He dropped them back into the sack and cleared his throat. "What do you think our chances are of Flanagan letting us leave camp tonight?"

Chris shrugged, then turned his gaze to Ephraim. "Why? Anywhere specific in mind?"

"The Taylor place."

"Any specific reason?"

He bounced the sack in his hand. "I imagine it's been a good while since they've enjoyed any sweets like these. They should have a happy Christmas after all they've been through."

"That's all?" Chris asked with reluctance.

Ephraim turned and looked him straight on. "If you must know, I intend on courting her."

Chris nearly spit out the muddy chicory and rye concoction he drank. "You *what*?"

"I want to court her."

At this Chris carried on, coughing and choking on the liquid. "Court *Miss Taylor*? You do remember that this was the woman who likely would've shot you if given the chance the first time you met?"

"I'll never know unless I ask."

Chris sucked in a deep breath and released it with a shake of his head. "You're mighty optimistic."

"Don't we have to be in our line of work?" Ephraim grinned and set off to find Captain Flanagan.

Through the hovering fog before them, a faint glow illuminated the night as though bidding them to draw closer. Ephraim nudged Shenandoah to go faster. It seemed an eternity had passed since he had been to the farm or seen its inhabitants.

At last the fog gave way to the scene he had dreamed of visiting again if only for a moment. The old house stood like a dear old friend, windows aglow with the warmth and tenderness only a family could give it. Tempest nickered from the barn, assuring that all was well. They paused just shy of the clearing, and searched for the familiar assuring glow of the two candles within the kitchen window.

The bone-weariness fell away as Ephraim caught sight of the signal. All was well.

Chris nudged him. "Are you going to ask tonight?"

Ephraim nudged Shenandoah forward. "Maybe." He dismounted and lashed the reins to the porch rail. Taking the steps two at a time, he slid his hat off and gripped it tightly in one hand, smoothing down the mess he knew existed on top of his head.

Chris cleared his throat in annoyance. "You look fine, Romeo."

"That's not what I — "

"Of course it wasn't," Chris said, wholly unconvinced. He brushed past him with a side glance and knocked three times.

The sound of footsteps inside grew closer, then the door was opened to reveal Pastor Taylor.

He motioned for them to come in out of the cold. Ephraim searched the room for Gideon, but he wasn't there. "Is Gideon all right?"

Mrs. Taylor, who had been at the fire busily stirring a simmering pot, touched his arm lightly. "He's just fine. Come and see."

They ducked into the side room. Gideon was propped up in bed, having his ear talked off by Benjamin. His face, though still pale and under-toned with pain, was happy. Relief washed over Ephraim. He hadn't realized how much Gideon meant to him. That was never supposed to happen. He hadn't wanted a family. Gideon was only a burden, or that was what he would've said only a month ago. But then again, none of this was supposed to have happened. He had somehow managed to find himself with a new young dependent in Gideon and, if he was lucky, a sweetheart in Mariah.

Mrs. Taylor swept past the bed and placed a hand on Benjamin's shoulder. "Let's go see if Papa needs help decorating the tree."

Ephraim stepped to the side to allow them to pass, then walked farther into the room. His pulse had started to increase and his heart felt as though it would give out. The form of his Bible could be felt through his coat. Emotions from the past that had haunted him for so long were now at the forefront of his mind. Maybe now that part of him that had never healed could finally be at ease.

Gideon smiled at him. It seemed to take every bit of strength he had, but he was smiling. Ephraim eased onto the edge of the bed.

"Did we whup 'em?"

Ephraim smiled wearily. "Something like that."

"I knew we would. Them Yankees don't have a chance, do they?"

"They ran like a polecat with a bur under its tail," Ephraim winked.

A fit of coughing came over Gideon. His face contorted into a twist of agony. When it had passed, he lay back against the pillows. "Don't tell Miss Taylor," he whispered. "She'll make me drink her bitter tea."

Ephraim laughed. "I wouldn't dream of it. I was once the recipient of that concoction, remember?" He pulled the candy pouch from his pocket and held it out toward Gideon. "Would a piece of this make it better?"

Light kindled in his eyes as he chose a piece of candy and popped it in his mouth. "Where did you get it," he asked, incredulous.

"That's a story for another time," Ephraim replied.

Gideon nodded and blinked wearily. "Did you see the lights?"

Ephraim's mind flashed back to the horrible slaughter of the battle. The smoke rising from the ruins of Fredericksburg, the bodies strewn across the Heights, the blood that soaked the Virginia soil, and the strange lights that seemed to reflect it all. "Yes, I saw them."

"Miss Taylor said it was a sign from Heaven."

Ephraim cocked his head. "What type of a sign?"

"To remind us that the Almighty is still in control." Gideon closed his eyes, as if even speaking stole strength from him.

The Almighty is still in control.

How many times had he questioned that in the previous year? Maybe all of this — Gideon, the lights, the chance meeting with Mariah — was just a reminder that God truly was in control.

"I have a gift for you," Ephraim said. He pulled his Bible from his other pocket and placed it on Gideon's lap.

"But it was your —"

Ephraim cleared his throat and stood before Gideon could finish his sentence. "For safe keeping. Flanagan said you'll be staying with the Taylors now. I figure you'll make sure it's taken care of until I come back."

"How long will you be gone?"

"You should know a scout can never tell these things," Ephraim said.

Gideon looked back to the Bible. His hands slowly opened it, gaze resting on the writing in the front. Another name had been added since he'd seen it last.

Gideon Bryant.

Ephraim knelt down beside the bed. "You know something? I think maybe God knows we need to be each other's family."

At this Gideon's face glowed with light, in spite of his apparent pain. "Family?"

"Well you've been my charge long enough in the Scouts. I reckon there's nothing so different about being my little brother. Unless you have a problem with taking the name Bryant as your own."

Gideon closed his eyes, a smile resting contentedly on his face. "*Gideon Bryant.* I knew God would answer my prayer, Sergeant," he whispered sleepily. "A family for Christmas …"

Ephraim choked back the lump forming in his throat. He was beginning to understand things in a different light. God wasn't asking him to forget the pain of losing his family. He was asking him to trust that it was with a purpose. He was asking him to live again.

Gideon yawned, eyelids appearing heavy. Ephraim stole quietly out of the room.

Chapter Fifteen

The warm glow of the fire illuminated the room where the Christmas tree stood in the corner, boasting its new ornaments, and the candles gleamed in the window.

Mrs. Taylor looked up, a question on her face. Ephraim threw a glance over his shoulder into the room again. "He's sleeping."

At this, her expression relaxed into a soft smile. "He's past the worst of it, I believe."

Something inside of Ephraim released — as if his soul could breathe again. Nothing could ever change his loss, but he was beginning to realize that God could still heal his heartache. Maybe it was time to finally rest.

A gush of cold air flooded the room as Benjamin came through, bringing a flurry of snow with him. His face was flushed with color brought about by the chilly night air. In his hands he struggled to carry a guitar.

"Will you play for us?" He held the instrument out with hopefulness in his eyes.

Ephraim furrowed his brow. "Where did you manage to find a guitar?"

Benjamin looked hesitantly toward Chris, who coughed into his fist guiltily.

Ephraim raised an eyebrow. He should've known that Chris would somehow manage to facilitate such a thing. He likely didn't want to know how he had done it.

Ephraim filled his lungs to capacity and took the guitar. He plucked the strings lightly, adjusting the tuning as he went. But when it was time to arrange the notes into a carol it was as though he couldn't will his fingers to move.

Chris cleared his throat and began to sing, filling the awkward moment. The first several lines quavered on their own before being joined by the mellow chords of the guitar.

"'And ye beneath life's crushing load, whose forms are bending low, who toil along the winding road with painful steps and slow, look now for glad and happy hours come swiftly on the wing. O rest beside the weary road and hear the angels sing.'"

Late into the night they continued their caroling, feasting on Ephraim's meager supply of candy, until finally conceding that it was time for sleep. The candles had whittled down to short stubs and the coals in the fireplace twinkled slowly.

Ephraim and Chris stood nearly in unison, shifting directions toward the door.

"Thank you for seeing Gideon is cared for," Ephraim said with a nod.

Pastor Taylor brushed away the words. "It's what any Christian folk would do." He joined them near the door, looking out into the heavily falling snow. "It's late and cold enough to freeze a man's blood solid. There's no use in you boys going out in it tonight. Why don't you stay?"

"Yes, you must," Mrs. Taylor insisted. "And tomorrow you'll keep Christmas with us."

A thunderous pounding on the door shattered the sleepy quiet of the house and startled Ephraim from his dreams. He threw back the blanket covering him and scrambled to his feet. Chris was close behind. They reached for their pistols and approached the door, peering out from the curtained window beside it.

Pastor Taylor appeared at the base of the stairs, wiping the sleep from his eyes. Only the Almighty knew what would bring someone to the farm so early on Christmas morning. Ephraim braced himself for the possibility that the Yanks had returned to take Pastor Taylor into custody again, or maybe somehow word had reached them that he and Chris were here.

"Bryant! McCammon!"

Ephraim slid the bolt on the door, allowing it to swing open, ushering in the cold wind that whipped through the valley. Armand stood breathless at the door. He bent to regain his breath.

"Flanagan's gathering the Scouts. Hear tell we're joining a raid with Stuart."

"Any idea where?" Ephraim asked.

Armand shrugged. "Nope. But Flanagan wants us ready to move soon."

"We'll saddle up and meet you back at camp."

Ephraim released a sigh as he watched Armand gallop into the snowy landscape. War didn't even stop for Christmas. But he had served under Stuart for a time, prior to joining the Scouts. If he knew the cavalry commander, even in the slightest, this would be a raid he wouldn't want to miss.

Chris had already pulled on his boots and coat, and headed out to brave the wintery sleet coming down. Ephraim turned to find somber faces gathered near Pastor Taylor. It was evident they had heard the news.

"I'll gather supplies for you to take," Mrs. Taylor said.

Ephraim nodded in gratitude. He pulled on his boots and slipped quietly into the room where Gideon slept. The blanket rose and fell peacefully with the boy's soft breathing. Heaviness settled over Ephraim. He never thought he would actually miss the kid. But he was finding out just how much he was going to.

He pulled the blanket up higher over his shoulders, and tucked it in lightly. Gideon stirred, blinking at him in the dim light.

Ephraim forced a smile of reassurance. "Go back to sleep. I was just making sure you were warm enough."

Gideon yawned. "Are you leaving?"

"Gotta give the Yankees a Christmas greeting. But I'll be back, and when I am, I'll expect to see you much improved."

It seemed Gideon only partly heard his words. He closed his eyes, a small smile resting on his face. Ephraim lingered for a moment.

Lord, watch out for him while I'm gone. If you are going to give me a family, you'll have to keep them safe in my absence.

"Sergeant," Mariah's soft voice entered his thoughts. "Shenandoah is ready."

He sucked in a breath and made his way into the frozen morning. Puffs of frost formed in the air. Shenandoah nickered as he readied her and followed Chris into the barnyard. He glanced up as a swath of light poured from the front door. Mariah and Pastor Taylor stood waiting for them on the porch.

Ephraim pulled tightly on his gloves and brushed off the front of his jacket. His heart accelerated its rhythm madly and his mouth went dry.

"Well, don't just stand there," Chris hissed. "This is your chance. Do you want her for a sweetheart or don't you?"

"Don't pressure me." Ephraim bit his lip, gaze unmoved from the two figures illuminated in the night.

"Hmph. If it wasn't for me you'd still be watching from a distance, convincing yourself you don't care for any of them, when in fact you do."

Ephraim didn't attempt a response. A man couldn't argue with truth. But he wasn't about to admit it out loud either. He dragged in a deep breath. Part of him would rather face a whole posse of Yankees than do what he was about to. Reconnaissance, battle, bullets, and artillery fire – they all seemed much easier to charge into.

Pull yourself together, Bryant. You're a scout. Your nerves are supposed to be impenetrable.

Now if only he actually believed it. He vowed he would never grow close to anyone again. Could he open himself up to the possibility of pain again?

Chris nudged him forward, and for a moment Ephraim thought about turning back around. But it was too late. They had both seen him now.

"Sergeant," Pastor Taylor said.

Ephraim cleared his throat and willed his legs to carry him forward. Each step felt as though he was on uneven ground, legs apt to buckle under him at any moment.

"Sir," he nodded.

"I put the supplies Mama gathered in your saddlebag," Mariah said. Her gaze moved beyond him to where Chris waited with the horses. "Our family will be praying for your safety."

Ephraim searched the path of trodden snow beneath him. "I hope you speak for more than just your family." He looked up to meet her eyes. Color flushed her face.

"Before I go... I..." He cleared his throat and started again. "I just wanted to say, I know I'm not well spoken like a man oughta be for this, but—"

"Spit it out, son," Pastor Taylor said.

"Miss Taylor, I'd sure be proud to know — what I mean is, I'd be honored if..." Ephraim dropped his head, heat rising to his face. "Would you wait for me?"

For a fleeting moment all was silent. To Ephraim, it was as though the world had stopped turning. He cringed inwardly. This wasn't going the way he had hoped.

"Are you asking to court me, Sergeant Bryant?"

"If you're agreeable. Your father gave his blessing last night."

Mariah gazed out toward the snowy landscape and hugged her shawl closer around her body. What was it she was thinking? Maybe he had jumped to conclusions regarding her affections.

The familiar old walls of thorns and briars that guarded his heart fought to regain the hold they once maintained. Maybe he was foolish to ever have removed them. He gripped his hat tightly.

"I'm agreeable, Sergeant Bryant. Though your manners are nothing to speak of," she said, her eyes aglow with teasing. "But promise me you'll come back safe."

The fireplace crackled, showering sparks up the chimney. Mariah gazed into the colored flames. Orange, yellow, blue. In the glowing coals and ashes she saw the remains of Fredericksburg. Those scenes would never leave her. Of that she was certain. Perhaps she didn't want them to. The haunting days she had lived through in the battle made God's hand even more clear. She closed her eyes and soaked up the warmth of the flames. Peace rolled over her soul, sweeping away the worries and cares of tomorrow and the war that still raged.

"'Peace I leave with you, my peace I give unto you: not as the world giveth, give I unto you. Let not your heart be troubled, neither let it be afraid.'"

It was the purpose of Christmas in one verse. Just as those present at the manger found rest in the dark of night, she could find rest in the midst of war. She was learning, as Ma Fletcher had said, that peace wasn't dependent on the circumstances in which she found herself. It was dependent on the Savior she leaned on.

Will you wait for me?

The question echoed through the corridors of Mariah's heart. Though peace on earth had reigned for a night, the war raged again. It held no hope for the future. Yet if their meeting was through the hand of Providence, surely *their* future was bright.

Look now, for glad and golden hours come swiftly on the wing. Oh rest beside the weary road, and hear the angels sing.

Did you enjoy this book?

Thank you, dear reader, for allowing me to paint this story on the canvas of your imagination. It is my hope that you have enjoyed *Rest Beside The Weary Road* as much as I enjoyed writing it. If you did, I would be honored if you would consider leaving a review at the place where you purchased it, or on Goodreads. Even a short review will help other readers, like you, discover Ephraim and Mariah's story.

The Carols of Christmas

In Thy Tender Care
by Courtney Ranger

Watch of Wand'ring Love
by Kendall Hoxsey

Rest Beside The Weary Road
by A. M. Watson

So, To Honor Him
by Alice Monday

Raise the Song on High
by DaLeena Taylor

Beneath the Guiding Star
by Sara A. Thren

And the Mountains in Reply
by Sienna Peake

Of Peace on Earth
by Abigail Kay

A Thrill of Hope
by Kellyn Roth

Author's Note

The War Between the States is a topic of heated debate. Discussions regarding the Confederacy's reasons for seceding and whether they had a right to secede are often brought to the table.

It is reasonable, then, that some who read these pages may wonder why the author has chosen to write from a Confederate point of view. The depth of the subject does not afford me the space here to expound fully on my decision to do so. However, due to the nature of the setting I have chosen, I would like to make clear my stance regarding the topic.

The first issue that is always brought up in a discussion regarding the War Between the States is, of course, that of slavery. First, let me be very clear. Slavery is a blight on any nation, and I fully condemn it. There is a misconception that is commonplace within debates on the topic that portrays all supporters of the Confederacy to be racist. I can assure you that this is not true.

It is the author's stance that, while slavery was a problem the states were sorting through at the time of the war, it was not the cause for the war. This is corroborated by the following quotes:

> "If you bring these [Confederate] leaders to trial, it will condemn the North, for by the Constitution secession is not rebellion."
>
> Chief Justice Salmon P. Chase, July 1867

> "The contest is really for empire on the side of the North, and for independence on that of the South, and in this respect we recognize an exact analogy between the North and the Government of George III, and the South and the Thirteen Revolted Provinces. These ... opinions are the general opinions of the English nation."
>
> London Times, November 7, 1861

> "The Union government liberates the enemy's slaves as it would the enemy's cattle, simply to weaken them in the coming conflict . . . The principle is not that a human being cannot justly own another, but that he cannot own him unless he is loyal to the United States."

The London Spectator with regard to the Emancipation Proclamation, October 11, 1862

It is important to note that Great Britain abolished slavery nearly thirty years before the start of the war, and had been pressuring America to do the same. This adds a depth of credibility to the quotes from these British newspapers. They were viewing the war and its causes through an unbiased perspective, and acknowledged that slavery was not the reason for the Confederacy's secession.

Many Confederate leaders themselves also testified to the real reason they fought.

> "We are not fighting for slavery. We are fighting for independence."
> Jefferson Davis, President of the CSA

> "It is said slavery is all we are fighting for, and if we give it up we give up all. Even if this were true, which we deny, slavery is not all our enemies are fighting for. It is merely the pretense to establish sectional superiority and a more centralized form of government, and to deprive us of our rights and liberties."
> Major General Patrick R. Cleburne, January 1864

It is my hope that you, my dear readers, will be inspired to study into the matter for yourselves. Go to the pages of history, and let it write its story on your heart.

Historical Note

Although the characters of *Rest Beside The Weary Road* are fictional, many of the places and events represented are not. It has been the author's desire to remain as close to historical accuracy as possible while still creating an engaging fictitious tale that will captivate the reader. To differentiate between historical facts and the author's creative license, a list of historical facts portrayed in this novella is provided below.

Bible Smuggling During The War

During the War Between the States, the Confederacy really did experience a mass shortage of Bibles, as portrayed in this novella. This shortage was due to multiple factors.

In the 1860s it was not common for households to own multiple copies of the Word of God. Each home typically had one or two copies. This presented a dilemma for the Confederacy when war broke out because many households sent their only copy of the

Bible with the men leaving for battle. At the time, the majority of printing presses were located in the northern states. This, combined with the lack of raw materials, such as ink, paper, and leather, meant that Bibles could not simply be printed to satiate the high demand for them in the Confederacy.

In 1861, James Graves, a prominent Baptist minister in the south, saw the need for Bibles and set out to smuggle a set of printing plates into the Confederacy for the purpose of printing them.

> "The North has no monopoly on the Word of God."
>
> James Graves

He was successful in smuggling the plates past the Union blockade and started printing pocket sized Bibles in Nashville, Tennessee. However, when the city fell to Union hands in February of 1862, Graves was forced to flee.

The Confiscation Acts, passed by Congress and signed into law by Lincoln, also played a crucial role in adding to the Bible shortage in the south. It prohibited Bibles from being passed through the Union blockade and classified them as contraband of war, subject to be confiscated. The American Bible Society tried in vain to facilitate the shipment of Bibles to the Confederacy. These attempts were immediately dismantled by the Lincoln Administration. They would not be deterred, however, and began a system of relaying Bibles to smaller Bible Societies in the border states. From there, the Bibles would be smuggled past the blockade, by people like the Taylors and Ma Fletcher, and make their way to the Confederate soldiers and civilians who so desperately longed for them.

So severe was the need, that a convention was held in Augusta, Georgia in 1862 with the intent to determine a solution for the printing and distribution of Bibles.

> "RESOLVED, That in the opinion of this Convention, the organization of a BIBLE SOCIETY, of the Confederate States of America, for the circulation of the Holy Scriptures, without note or comment, in our own and in foreign lands, is imperatively demanded; and should be secured at the earliest practical moment."
>
> Proceedings of the Bible Convention of the Confederate States of America

In his book, *A History of Book Publishing in the United States*, John Tebbel wrote on the topic, "The Bible shortage in the Confederate States of America is so severe that Union prisoners in Richmond, Va. were selling their copies for up to $15.00 each in order to buy food." It is important to note that the modern monetary equivalent, as of the time this novella was published, would be over $300.00. This shows how desperate the Confederacy was for the Word of God.

The Confederate Scouts

The Confederacy was renowned for being well ahead of its times in the realm of clandestine operations. Major players in this regard were, of course, the infamous groups of partisan Rebel scouts. While Flanagan and his band of Scouts are entirely fictitious, they are inspired by groups like John Mosby's Rangers, the Coleman Scouts, and Wade Hampton's Iron Scouts. These courageous groups of men carried out daring raids and missions against the Union that earned them fierce reputations. They were heralded as bands of dashing heroes by the Confederate civilians they protected. Yet to the Union troops who clashed with them, they were formidable forces who were not to be reckoned with.

It has been said that the Confederate scouts carried all the daring and intrigue of Robin Hood, and were the forerunners of our modern-day Black Op forces.

The Aurora Borealis

The Aurora Borealis is the last thing that many of us think about when we think of Virginia. However, on the evening of December 13, 1862, the hauntingly beautiful lights dazzled the skies above the Fredericksburg battlefield. It was a phenomenon never seen before by many who found themselves in the middle of the war's chaos. For some it seemed to be an omen of terrible things yet to come. Others believed it was a haunting tribute to the blood spilled on Fredericksburg's heights that night, or a celebration of Confederate victory. Still others, like Mariah and Ephraim, felt it was a reminder that God presided over the affairs of men.

The reason for the lights, at the end of such a bloody battle, is a mystery known but to God. However it is of a truth that nothing happens without purpose. Perhaps the Almighty truly did want to remind mankind that he is ever in control.

Christmas During The War

Christmas in Virginia during the War Between the States looked much different than it does today. The war meant that many homes and firesides were missing husbands, fathers, sons, and brothers. Sugar and sweets were scarce, there were no feasts and lavish parties, and most gifts were quite simple. Yet, in spite of their circumstances, soldiers and civilians alike still found ways to celebrate the season.

It was not unheard of, during the Christmas of 1862, for soldiers to take part in their own unofficial truces. Sometimes they would meet half way between their respective posts and exchange supplies. Items like coffee, tobacco, and candy would be traded. In these moments, for a short time, peace embraced men who otherwise might have been killing each other. Tally

Simpson, a Confederate soldier camped near Fredericksburg in 1862, wrote home to his sister, "When will this war end? Will another Christmas roll around and find us all wintering in camp? Oh! That peace may soon be restored to our young but dearly beloved country and that we may all meet again in happiness."

Stuart's Christmas Raid

In the final scene, the Flanagan Scouts are ordered back to camp in order to participate in a raid involving J.E.B. Stuart and his cavalry. This Christmas Raid of 1862 really did take place. Stuart took 1,800 cavalrymen and a battery of horse artillery into Union-held territory with the orders from General Lee stating, "penetrate the enemy's rear, ascertain if possible his position & movements, & inflict upon him such damage as circumstances will permit."

From this raid came a rather humorous quote. Upon capturing an enemy telegraph line, Stuart sent a message to the Union Quartermaster in the area. It stated, "General Meigs will in the future please furnish better mules; those you have furnished recently are very inferior."

The raid proved to be of no dramatic impact for the Confederacy. However, it did remind the Union that no place in Virginia was beyond the Confederate Cavalry's reach.

Acknowledgements

Time and space would fail me the opportunity to adequately thank all those who played a role in the creation of this novella, but there are some that I would like to thank especially.

To my amazing family, you are the best support system an author could ever ask for. Thank you for bearing with me through the messiness of plotting, drafting, dreaming, and yes, sometimes screaming. The late-night banter as we worked through plot-holes, the dinner table discussions about the historical setting, and the many prayers through this process on my behalf have been invaluable. It has been a year of trial and growth for us, but I believe God intended for this story to be told in the midst of it all. After all, "peace is not found in what's around you. It's found in *Who's* within you."

To the Morenos, your encouragement has pushed me to reach for the heights. Thank you for coming with me on this journey. I pray God blesses you immensely for your kindness and support.

To Madi, thank you for your support and for always being willing to answer my many questions. Your knowledge and helpful spirit are a true gift. I'm honored to call you a friend.

Above all, I join the Heavenly Host in proclaiming, "glory to God in the highest".

Meet The Author

A. M. Watson is a daughter of the King — ransomed, redeemed, and justified by the blood of Jesus Christ. Born with the wind in her soul, she loves the prairie and listening at night to the lonesome howl of the coyotes. An ardent believer in teaching the past to the future generations, she desires to instill a love for history in those who read her stories. Her passion is penning tales of redemption, patriotism, and hope through history's greatest storms. When she's not writing, she can be found studying deeper into history, playing instruments, and drinking lots of coffee.

Want to connect? Head over to linktr.ee/a.m.watson

Made in the USA
Coppell, TX
27 February 2026

72464734R00125